CW01431073

Betrayed by The Pack

An Omegaverse Reverse Harem Romance

Layla Sparks

Copyright © 2023 by Layla Sparks

All rights reserved.

No portion of this book may be reproduced in any form without written permission from the publisher or author, except as permitted by U.S. copyright law.

Contents

Omegaverse Terms

A few things to know regarding the omegaverse world. The people in the omegaverse display a more canine or wolflike behavior. Some books involve shifting into wolves. This series will have minimal to no shifting.

Here are some terms that will be helpful to know (*note: these definitions pertain to my stories):

Omega: A female or male who would often have multiple partners to help them during heats. Usually has a particular scent that alphas find very appealing and unable to resist.

Beta: Like a normal human

Alpha: Top of the food chain, and they gravitate to omegas. They also have a scent to attract omegas.

Delta: Ferocious and deadly, typically guards and second in command to alphas

Slick: Secretion from the privates

Heat: A period where an omega needs to mate - akin to ovulating in human females.

Knot: When an alpha mates an omega— and the base of the penis swells, locking the alpha and omega in place for impregnation

Rut: Alphas can go into rut phase, similar to heat. Sometimes an omega's heat will bring it on.

Scent blockers: Can come in pills or as a cream. Blocks an omega scent from attracting alphas.

Heat Suppressants: Stops an omega from going into heat

Trigger Warnings: Mention of miscarriage, Child Kidnapping, Pregnancy, Backdoor Play

Content Guide

If you don't have any triggers, please skip this page to avoid spoilers!

For any questions regarding triggers, please email: author_ laylasparks@yahoo.com.

- Double Penetration

- Menage

- Group Play

- Backdoor (anal) Play

- Kidnapping (forced pleasuring - chapter 26)

- Pregnancy

- Domestic Discipline/ Spanking

- Claiming bites

For readers who prefer not to read about pregnancy or babies, please skip the bonus epilogue.

Prologue

Vanessa

"Take her," ordered King Armon.

My life seemed to be crumbling before my eyes. My hands wrapped protectively over my pregnant belly. King Armon had just announced he would put me up for auction after my baby was born.

And the Royal Pack would keep the baby.

I studied his face to see if he was serious, and he looked like he was. It was *his* daughter that I helped get kidnapped, after all. I should have never trusted Voss. He was only watching out for himself. I had told him where Princess Lyra would be so he could kidnap her for a remote village, gain his people's trust, and take over the kingdom.

I didn't think he'd *actually* try to kill her.

The room seemed to spin after King Armon gave his final verdict. I couldn't believe it. Maybe I deserved it.

The guards grabbed my arms, and I didn't have the strength to fight them as they walked me down the stairs. *Was I going to live in the dungeons now?*

Everything got darker and darker the further down we walked. Fear gripped my heart as they opened a cell door as if I was a prisoner. There was nothing but a bare dirty mattress on the stone floor.

"Are you serious?" I shouted at them. They shoved me inside and shut the door, locking it behind them.

Without a word, the two guards clomped up the stairs. I was still gripping the cold metal bars by the time the deathly silence reigned around me. The steady drip drip of water above me and the howl of the cold gust of air swirling around were frightening.

"Let me go!" I screamed again, shaking the bars.

After all my hard work and determination to climb the social ladder, this is where I would end up in. Tears burned in my eyes as I released the cold metal bars. The darkness around me was overwhelming, and I shut my eyes tight. Maybe I was in a nightmare.

I opened my eyes, still seeing that I was trapped down here. I lifted my dress as I walked towards the filthy mattress on the ground.

My dress was drenched at the edges as I gingerly sat cross-legged on the mattress. I rubbed my hand over my belly protectively. I had to get the hell out of here with my baby intact. The Royal Pack would *not* take my baby. Especially if my baby was going to be raised by the old hag Queen Ophelia.

I did nothing but try to better my life after meeting King Armon at the Omega Ball last year. I remembered the night as if it was yesterday...

"Stand up straight bitch," said Aunt Helen. Aunt Helen took me in when I was twelve, after my parents died during the Great Moon Revolt. She was strict along with my Uncle Gabe.

I straightened my shoulders as we walked into the Omega Ball. I never saw anything like it. Lights and chandeliers everywhere. Musicians were playing their instruments, and there were beautiful people everywhere.

I swallowed with nervousness.

I had to impress an alpha pack, or else I'd have to go home with my aunt and uncle tonight. I fucking hated them. The isolation and the lonely little closet they'd put in me were too much to bear. I needed out, and I would do anything to get an alpha's attention tonight.

And I did.

The night at the Omega Ball was the most magical fucking night of my life. The kings had fallen for me, and despite the existing omega in their relationship, they still took me in with open arms. They secretly courted me one by one, even though rumors about us were spread all over Howl's Edge island.

All they wanted was a child that their omega wife couldn't provide.

But now...they were going to take *my* child.

***

The days and nights passed as I stayed huddled on the mattress. My pregnancy was advancing day by day, and I still hadn't found a way out of this cell. My body felt increasingly tired, but the urgency to escape grew like fire in my heart.

I had to find a way out for my baby and I.

I couldn't tell when it was night or day anymore.

I only knew the time of the day when the maid would bring me my meals. It was the only way I kept track of the days passing by. Dirty plates were stacked up in the corner of the cell, and a loose plan was formulating in my brain. Maybe there could be a way out of here after all.

"Your breakfast, ma'am," said the beta maid shakily, handing my plate through a small slot between the bars. I lazily lay on the mattress, one hand on my swollen belly.

"My back hurts, and I can barely move," I groaned, my hand moving to my lower back. "Could you please be a dear and bring in my food? Also, there's a ton of dirty plates here, and I can't stand the smell."

I covered my nose weakly, pretending to retch, but nothing came out. The beta maid stood there uncertainly and then shook her head.

"Of course, I will pick those up right away," she said. "I feel so bad they put a pregnant omega in these conditions."

My stomach leaped excitedly as she unlocked the cell door using a large ring of keys. When the door swung open, I had to keep the look of jubilation off my face, still pretending to act weak for her to trust me. She slowly set the plate of food in front of me and then proceeded to walk over to the dirty plates in the corner of the cell. As soon as I saw her bending down to grab the plates, I gathered up my dress and made a dash for it.

"What are you doing?" she yelled.

I shut the cell door behind me. I didn't dare look back as I ran up the stairs. My legs felt weak, but this was for my life. My legs burned with every step on these dreadful stairs.

This was my last chance.

My heart pounded hard in my chest as I reached the top step. I heard the cell door squeak open as she chased after me. She grabbed my ankle somehow.

"Please," I begged quietly. "They'll kill me."

She blinked and then opened her mouth to scream. I kicked her hard in the face, and she fell backward, knocked out cold on the ground. That bitch was going to let me die anyway.

My legs pumped under me as I dashed through the hallways and out the back door to the terrace. The sun hit me in the face as I ran towards the graveyard. I knew there was a way out of this compound through there. It was early in the morning, with the sun nearly blinding me. I hadn't seen the sun in days.

I couldn't believe I was finally outside.

I took a breath of fresh air as I ran wildly past the trees and the graveyard. I heard bells ringing behind me and shouts in the air.

The Royal Pack knew I escaped. There were guards perched everywhere who could have seen me running across the fields.

I could barely catch my breath as I ran faster out of the compound.

As I ran into the streets, people were giving me odd looks here and there. I had no idea where I was going, but I knew I had to leave Howl's Edge now. I couldn't stay here any longer.

I kept running and stopped when I felt a stitch at my side. I looked around and saw the palace guards from afar scanning the area for me, guns out. I ran behind one of the luxury diamond stores, shutting my eyes and just praying they wouldn't think to look over here.

Supply planes left every Tuesday, and my brain whirled with plans to escape Howl's Edge for good.

Chapter 1

Three Years Later

Vanessa

"**D**amn," I muttered as I drove around the parking lot, trying to find a spot. The little strip club barely had parking, and the customers would park in our employee section. "Ugh, that'll have to do."

I was already late to work, and I knew my boss would freak out on me. He literally timed when I would come in to work next.

Stepping out of the car, I nearly tripped over a pothole, wearing my tall silver heels with straps around my ankles. I wore a sleek silver bodysuit paired with black high-waisted leggings. The bodysuit was backless with a plunging neckline, showing just enough cleavage. My hair was done in long pigtails which swung over my silver hoop earrings.

As I walked down the street, the smell of smog was overwhelming. Its thick, acrid scent burned the back of my throat and stung my eyes. Cars and buses honked their horns and roared past me. When I finally reached the establishment, I groaned, seeing that it was already full of human males inside, considering it was my night to dance. The *Red Light Lounge* was too small to host many customers, but the manager didn't seem to mind the booming business since I started. A human male was no match for an omega's charms.

I walked around to the back of the building.

"About time," called Bruce.

He was standing outside the doors, waiting eagerly for me. He was the manager of the strip club. A tall, broad-shouldered man. He was in his late 40s, with salt-and-pepper hair, a thick mustache, and impeccably dressed in a tailored suit and tie.

He had found me lost and alone in the streets, taking me in like a lost puppy. When first arriving at the human lands, I was scared to death but soon found my way around it with Bruce's help. He had taken me in until I could move out on my own, but in return, I'd work for him here. I didn't mind the dancing, but I didn't want to do this for the rest of my life.

Living paycheck to paycheck was hard sometimes, and I wanted a better life for my three-year-old son.

"Sorry," I said, flipping my long red hair out of my eyes. "The babysitter was late."

I didn't have a choice but hire the cheapest help I could find. The teen babysitter relied on her parents for a ride to my apartment. My son loved her, so that was all that mattered.

"It's time to fire your babysitter," said Bruce gruffly. "The customers are waiting. I could already see the wads of cash in their hands."

"Alright, alright," I said, trying to move past him.

"Hold on a moment, honey," he said in a low voice, capturing my chin in his hand. I instantly turned away from him.

"We're not a thing anymore, Bruce," I said. "I meant it last week."

I had been sleeping with Bruce since he saved my ass while I lived in his house. Sex with a human wasn't exactly satisfying, but it helped when my omega self felt a little frisky. When I realized that he was starting to develop actual feelings- that was when it was time to pull away.

"We're not done talking about this," said Bruce, scratching his beard in frustration. "Go on in then."

Sighing, I walked into the establishment and was immediately hit by the smell of sweaty bodies and alcohol. Even from the back, I could smell it all. Going into the dressing room, which led directly out to the stage, I lowered my bodysuit down my chest to show more cleavage and adjusted my bra. The bra was black and glittery, which matched my leggings. I fluffed my hair and put on a fresh coat of red lipstick.

Smacking my lips in the mirror, I twirled, satisfied with my appearance.

My heart was beating in anticipation of the loud music in the club. Then, leaving my things in the dressing room, I took a deep breath and waited for the next song to start.

Once on the stage, I gyrated to the beat of the music as the strobe neon lights flashed over our bodies. I danced with three other women, but the males let out a giant cheer when I stepped onto the stage. The other women, dressed in nothing more than lingerie and high heels, seductively moved their bodies to the music while the men watched with hungry eyes. Letting the music take over me, I swung around the pole while staring at the crowd of men with hooded eyes. The door to the *Red Light Lounge* opened, and from the side of my eye, I noticed three males enter the room. Something about their entrance changed the energy in the room. Something didn't feel right.

My heart beating fast, I twirled around the pole and took a good look.

One of them was handsome as the devil himself. He had dark eyes, wavy black hair, and clear olive skin. He was broad-shouldered and imposing, his large frame dwarfing all the men. His eyes darted to me, and his mouth pulled up into a mischievous smile.

Heart pounding, I nearly slipped off the pole.

He was a fucking alpha.

Was he here to take me back to the Royal Pack? Did they send him here?

Chapter 2

Jack

"She's pretty hot," said Ryan, my beta pilot with glasses and shaggy blond hair. He had caught me checking out the beautiful dancer on stage.

"Indeed she is," I muttered into my cup as I watched her dance.

The fiery redheaded woman on stage caught my eye.

She had striking green eyes that sparkled in the stage lights, and her long wavy hair in pigtails cascaded down her sides in curls. She was tall and lean, with curves in all the right places.

God damn.

"I've never seen a human so captivating. Almost like an omega, would ya' say?" said Liam, who was a delta. He was the bodyguard of the group assigned to me from the Royal Pack.

"Mhm," I said, sipping on my bitter drink. When she took a break, she was immediately surrounded by thirsty human men demanding her attention. "I think I might go for a private dance."

"I thought your rule was not to have sex with human women," grunted Liam.

"I'm not having sex," I said. "Dude, it's just a dance."

Liam's face cracked into a wide smile. "Go ahead then. Play with fire, my man."

"Have fun, boss," said Ryan, laughing as he popped a cherry into his mouth and talked to a lonely girl at the bar looking at him with interest. Ignoring my pack, I headed to the redheaded beauty who was taking a sip from a drink.

"Hello," I greeted, sticking my hand out to shake hers. Her body shone with sweat mixed with glitter as she fanned herself.

"Hello there," she said breathlessly, shaking my hand. Her soft skin under my rough palm triggered my alpha senses. Awakening me. I looked closer into her eyes, and she looked away quickly, her cheeks turning a slight pinkish color.

"What's your name?" I said, keeping her hand in mine, so she didn't think of running away.

"It doesn't really matter, does it?" she said, one eyebrow pulled up in sarcasm. Then she looked over at a man wearing a suit. The man gave her a warning look, and she turned her gaze back to me somberly. He was probably her manager. "My name's Vanessa."

"May I get a private dance?" I asked.

She looked at me sharply. "How much?"

"A hundred," I said. She cocked her head to one side, her pigtail draping her pale arm. I then noticed the mark on her shoulder.

The mark of a wolf claw. The mark of an omega.

Shock went through my body, but I disguised it quickly, smiling smoothly. How the fuck hadn't I noticed right away? She must have been taking the scent blockers to the maximum. Why was she here and not at Howl's Edge? She had no business being in the human world, and frankly, she wasn't allowed to be here.

"That works," she said businesslike and not meeting my eyes at all. She hadn't noticed that I knew she was an omega. *Could she sense I was an alpha?* Probably not, because she was treating me like some random thirsty human. "Follow me."

She pulled her hand away from mine and led me behind a black curtain. There was a chair in the middle of the room, and she gestured for me to sit on the chair. With the song playing, she ran her fingers along my thigh while swaying her hips seductively to the music. Her eyes were focused on mine as she slowly unsnapped her bra. My breath hitched in my throat as I grasped both sides of the chair.

The glittering black bra dropped to the ground, and she covered her pale orbs with her hands. Then to the beat of the music, she released her breasts, swaying her large breasts in my face. I longed to pull her red nipple into my mouth. To suck her nipple until it pebbled. My dick hardened in my pants.

I shifted in my seat, trying to get closer to her.

"Can I touch you?" I asked.

"No," she replied. "You can only watch. That's the rule, baby."

Her hands went to my chest as I frustratingly tried to gain alpha control as she slowly traced over the contours of my muscles. Her hips gyrated to the slow sexy song in the background all the while. Teasing me. My dick was stone hard as she sat on my lap, grinding against me, her breasts bouncing to the music.

I craved to touch her.

As the song reached its climax, this mysterious omega wrapped her legs around my waist, pulling me even closer. Because I was so close to her physically, I was able to get a whiff of her omega perfume. A hint of cotton candy and roses. I couldn't help but trace my thumb against the back of her neck.

Her eyes widened, and the heat between us grew unbearable. I heard her sigh, then her shoulders stiffened.

She quickly jumped up and reached down to grab her abandoned bra.

"That enough for tonight," she said huskily. "Time to pay up, sir."

Chapter 3

Vanessa

I was flustered as I dabbed my face with a tissue walking to my car later that night.

I couldn't believe an alpha was here in freaking Nashville, Tennessee. I tried to choose a remote area, but the Royal Pack had found me anyway. It was time to leave and never come back. I didn't have a choice now. I had to quit my job.

If I returned to this job and saw the alphas again, they might discover I was an omega. That was the last thing I wanted. This was probably the impetus I needed to finally leave this job. I noticed my manager, Bruce, leaning against my car.

What the hell did he want now?

"What's up?" I asked nonchalantly. "I'm not getting fired, am I?"

He let out a sigh and looked up at the night sky. "I've been thinking about you, Vanessa."

My heart sank. This was bad.

"Like I said, it's over," I said. "It's not that serious. Plus, I have a kid. I wanted to talk to you about something, actually."

It was better now than never.

"Shoot."

"This will be my last night working here."

"Listen, don't leave," he said, his eyes frantic. "I'm sorry about what I said."

"No, it's not what you said," I said. "Actually, on second thought, it is. I can't handle this type of harassment. Can you move so I can get to my car?"

I tried to scoot past him, but he grabbed my arm.

"You're wild, Vanessa. I know you like it when I take charge," he said in a low voice. His mouth to my ear. Instead of feeling horny like I usually did when he took me roughly, my stomach twisted in disgust.

"Just stop," I whispered. "Bruce, I know you're a nice guy."

"I can't stop dreaming about you. Every fucking night," he groaned, pushing me up against the car. His mustache scratched my throat as he kissed my neck. "You have a hold on me that I can't explain. Please, baby."

"No," I said firmly, pushing against his chest, but he wasn't budging. "Bruce, I'm being for real."

"You heard the lady," growled a voice from the hood of my car.

Heart pounding, I looked up to see the alpha that I had given a lap dance, squatting on the hood of my car.

Ready to attack.

"She's my girl," said Bruce, not moving an inch from me. "I'm the manager of this place. Get the hell outta my property."

"She said no," said the alpha, his eyes as dark as night. The glow of his gold irises flashed in the moon. "Step away."

I shivered, feeling the alpha command in his voice. Bruce looked startled at the severity of the alpha's command, but he didn't release me.

"She's mine," said Bruce stubbornly.

"Bruce, you better run," I warned, unsure what the hell this alpha would do to him. It was in an alpha's nature to be the most dominant male in the room, and if they were protective of an omega, nothing would stand in their way.

"Fuck no," said Bruce. At his words, the alpha jumped off the car and tackled Bruce to the ground. He began punching him in the face repeatedly.

Until Bruce was unconscious on the ground.

"Don't kill him!" I shouted at the alpha.

The alpha hopped off Bruce's limp body and stood before me, not ruffled in the slightest except for a drop of blood on his shirt. My heart raced as he placed both arms on either side of me, trapping me against the car. He was unshaken, his black hair mussed with a few strands covering his eyes from his fight.

"What is an *omega* like you doing here?" he growled.

It was like a bomb erupted in my head. Everything that I had ever built on my very own would come crashing down.

He knew.

He knew I was a fucking omega this entire time. During the entire lap dance, he played me.

"What does it matter to you?" I spat out.

Behind him, his pack surrounded us, blocking any chance of escape for me. One was a beta with shaggy blond hair and large wide-rimmed glasses. The other looked like a delta, judging from his lean frame and muscular torso. I turned to look at the alpha holding me hostage with his powerful, wide frame. I could feel my weak omega body feel the pressure of his alpha presence.

The need to obey and surrender immediately.

"It matters because you're not allowed to be here," he said. "We will be taking you back home. Back to Howl's Edge."

"Please, no," I said. "Just pretend you never saw me here."

"My conscience won't allow that," he said. Then he looked curiously at me. "How long have you lived here in the human lands?"

"Years, and I've been doing just fine," I said adamantly, hoping I could talk my way out of this. "You really don't have to worry about me. What are *you* doing here, though?"

"I don't need to explain myself to you," he said. So he was one of *those* alphas. The ones who thought they were above everyone. "We'll be taking you back home. Name's Jack."

He stuck out his hand to shake mine, but I ignored it. Jack raised his eyebrows in surprise.

"Do we take her now?" asked the delta.

"Yep, might as well," said Jack. It was normal for alphas to control their omegas and ensure they weren't out of bounds. It was his duty to bring me back to Howl's Edge. Whether I liked it or not.

"I have a baby here," I begged. "Just let me get my baby and pack some of our things."

I had to buy some time before they hauled me out of here.

He cocked his head to one side. Studying me. "Alright then, we'll follow your car with ours. Any fishy business will get you transported immediately."

"Okay," I said quickly.

He released me, and I shakily got into my car, shutting the door in their faces.

I drove like a maniac down the road.

I weaved between cars and even passed red lights, but the alpha car behind me was quick on my tail. I pressed the gas pedal and drove around a corner, and a large truck came behind me, blocking them. Excited at the reprieve, I turned another corner in one of the back roads and lost the alpha and his pack.

I whooped out loud when I lost them. I couldn't go back to Howl's Edge.

The Royal Pack would claim the baby and dump me at the Omega Auctions. Letting out a sigh of relief, I took the long road back to my apartment. Hopefully, the babysitter wasn't asleep.

As I walked into my little apartment on shaky legs, the first thing I heard was the low hum of the TV. Then, walking into the living room, I saw the babysitter munching on snacks and watching a movie, her bare feet lying on my brown coffee table. Her long highlighted hair was a rat's nest, and she wore black sweatpants with a too-large black hoodie.

She looked up, surprised to see me there.

"Thank you for staying late, Sarah," I said.

"You're welcome," she said. "Anything not to go home and get bossed around by parents."

I would do anything to get my parents back.

"Your mom is waiting out front," I said. I had called her mother after the crazy car chase.

"Ugh," said Sarah. "Can't I just live here with you and Gabe? What happened to you? You're shaking."

"Nothing happened."

"So, can I live with you guys?"

"No, you know that won't be possible," I said. "If you lived with me, you wouldn't be up this late watching TV anyway. This isn't everyday life, trust me. How was Gabe?"

"He was good. He threw Cheerios all over the floor."

True enough, I saw the little brown ringlets thrown haphazardly all over my purple rug under the dining table. My three-year-old could be a monster sometimes despite his cuteness. He was a little copy of me, and I knew I was in for a long adventure raising that child.

After the babysitter left, I locked the front door and leaned against it, shaking like a leaf.

I was certain Jack and his pack were working for the Royal Pack. They had to be. *How else would they have found me?*

Jack meant danger. No matter how hot he was.

Walking into Gabe's room, I saw him sound asleep in his crib. His blond curls, a complete contrast from mine, framed his little face. His hair color was a reminder of the Royal Pack. His dad was one of the kings of Howl's Edge. I watched him take little fast breaths on his side, cuddling his fluffy toy shark which was squished underneath his tummy. I smiled and kissed Gabe on the cheek, being careful not to wake him up. I would do anything to protect my baby.

And that meant we had to move out of here.

I walked to my room, scavenging for a suitcase. I finally found one deep in the closet and started to throw underwear, bras, and baby clothes in it. I planned to go somewhere temporarily until the alpha pack got tired of looking for me, and then I'd return for the rest of my things.

It was the only way.

Chapter 4

Vanessa

The next morning, I woke up to a loud crash and a curse.

My heart pounding, I sat up in bed and heard noises coming from the living room.

Robbers.

I had to get to Gabe. Rushing out of bed, dizzy as hell, I ran across from my room into Gabe's. Locking the door behind me, I saw him already jumping up and down in his crib. I still heard noises coming from the living room, and my heart pounded in fear.

I cracked the door open an inch.

"Get the hell out of my home!" I screamed.

Men's laughter sounded in the living room. Furious, I closed Gabe's door behind me and tiptoed into the living room. My heart stopped when I saw who was sprawled out on my beige couch.

It was Jack and his pack sitting in my living room. And my vase of flowers was broken on the floor.

"Sorry about that," said the beta with the blond hair, scrambling to pick up the mess.

"Look who's awake," said Jack, smirking. His long legs stretched in front of him. The delta with the slicked-back brown hair and green eyes was also staring at me. I was suddenly self-conscious of my red silk pajama shorts and tank top. "Did you think you could hide from us? Especially after we know an omega is in town."

"What's so wrong with me staying here?" I asked, annoyed out of my mind. *Why won't they just leave me the fuck alone?* I wanted to slap the smirk off Jack's handsome face.

"It's not safe for an omega to be here by herself," said Jack. "Grab your things and your baby. We're leaving now."

"Don't tell me what to do," I said.

I was seething inside.

But I also craved being protected and taken care of by an alpha. Even though I had terrible experiences in the past with the Royal Pack, that was all I ever wanted. To be genuinely loved and protected for. But Jack was another alpha I had to watch out for, despite his devilishly handsome looks.

"We can do it the hard way then," said Jack, raising his eyebrows at my rudeness. "I'll have Liam here carry you to the car, and Ryan will bring your kid along. Easy peasy. Choose wisely."

I quietly stalked off to Gabe's room. He was crying now. He was afraid and alone while I was in the living room, fighting for our lives.

"I'm sorry, Gabey," I muttered, carrying him into my arms and kissing his chubby red cheeks. "Shh, my love, it's okay. Mommy's here."

Gabe sniffled and hiccuped, his tiny hands clutching at my shirt. "You left me," he said, his voice trembling.

"It's okay, I'm here now," I said, rubbing circles around his back. "We're going someplace special now with Mommy's friends."

"Where?"

"It's a surprise," I said, setting him down and finding him an outfit to wear.

Gabe and I sat in the backseat of a large SUV.

Liam was driving with Jack sitting next to him. The beta sat in the middle seat in front of us, constantly turning to play peek-a-boo with Gabe and making Gabe laugh uncontrollably.

I didn't know what to think.

This was an impossible situation to get out of. No one was giving me a straight answer about when exactly we'd go to Howl's Edge. We were driving past farmland, pretty far out from the city. I was upset and hadn't said a word for an hour.

"Why isn't she talking?" asked Jack.

"Vanessa has every right to be angry at you," said Ryan. "You literally tore her from her home."

I was grateful to Ryan for speaking up and coming to my defense. Of the entire group, I hated him the least.

"Thanks," I said in a low voice.

"Hey, no problem," said Ryan. "Do you need anything to drink for this long ride? I have water bottles up here."

"No thanks," I muttered, staring out the window at the large plots of land we drove by. My son squeezed my hand in his little ones. We were leaving behind everything I had ever built for my son and me. The little taste of the freedom I had was now gone.

"Are you sad, Mommy?" His inquisitive, bright green eyes didn't miss a thing. I could swear his intelligence level had to be above average for a kid his age.

"No, baby," I said. "I'm just sleepy."

"We're almost there," said Liam.

After another thirty minutes of driving, I gasped when I saw their house. It was enormous. Nothing like I'd ever seen. The house was tall and covered in large glass windows. The cobblestone driveway wound up to the house, surrounded by neatly trimmed hedges and shrubs.

I was the last to leave the van as I held Gabe's hand tightly. There was a large pool in the front of the house. I never taught him how to swim, and he was never around water like I had as a kid growing up next to the ocean of Howl's Edge. A pang of homesickness came over me. The palm trees and the sand under my feet. But at the same time, it was a place that I never wanted to step foot into again.

Walking into the actual estate was something else. The landscaped gardens were a lush tapestry of vibrant flowers, shady trees, and trickling fountains.

"It's beautiful," I muttered under my breath.

"I agree," said Jack, looking in my direction.

"It doesn't mean I'm okay with being kidnapped," I said, making sure he understood that loud and clear.

No matter how fancy his house was.

As we walked inside, I noticed the grand staircase with bronze banisters. It was simply stunning. I couldn't stop staring at everything. The magnificent high ceilings and the large fake palm tree in the corner. A white recliner was in the middle of the living room, with a cream-colored coffee table in the middle. A large flat-screen television sat high above the fireplace. There was a maid quietly setting up food on a majestic oak dining table that could easily seat sixteen people. After living in my small apartment for three years, this was a lot.

Even though I had lived in the Royal Palace before, it was still breathtaking to me, all the same. I loved nice things, even though sometimes it could be at the expense of others. I never forgot how much Queen Ophelia hated me when her husbands took me as their second omega because she couldn't have children anymore.

"I can show you to your room before we eat," said Jack. I silently followed Jack up the staircase while carrying my squirming three-year-old in my hands, who was starting to get fussy without his afternoon nap. I couldn't help but notice Jack's muscular ass as he walked up the stairs.

Jack opened the door to a room with a king-sized bed. It was a simple room with a white comforter and oversized pillows. The room had sheer white curtains and a large thick beige rug with circles on it. "This is our guest room. You'll be staying here until we can get you back home."

I nodded, not saying a word.

"You know- we're just trying to save your life," he continued as he leaned against the door. "You should be grateful we're bringing you back to your true home. You don't belong here."

Ignoring him, I sat Gabe on the floor and walked to the window. I noticed a large building in the back with a large white dome.

"What's that?" I asked.

"The greenhouse," he said after a slight pause.

"What's in it?"

"It's not important. Don't go in there," he said, sounding panicked.

I quietly turned away from the window to look him in the eyes. He was hiding something, and he looked guilty for some reason.

"When are we going to Howl's Edge?" I asked instead.

"In a few days," he said.

"You said you had some business to do first. What type of business?" I asked persistently.

He licked his lips.

"It's really not important, I promise you."

"What shady stuff are you doing?"

His lips twisted into a wry smile. "You won't stop, huh? It's a greenhouse."

"For?"

"For the plants used in omega heat suppressant pills and scent blocker creams."

"Aren't those illegal to just grow anywhere?" I asked. I was surprised to learn he was part of the drug rings that made a ton of money selling this shit behind closed doors.

"It's not illegal for me," he said. "The Royal Pack assigns certain people to grow these worldwide in hidden locations. That's why it should be kept secret."

"Oh," I said. "Well, your secret's safe with me."

"Why don't you unpack and come to lunch?"

"Alright," I said, my stomach growling when he mentioned lunch. Jack chuckled and left the room. I sat cross-legged next to Gabe, who was hiding under the bed and ripping books underneath it. "Please, Gabe. Come on out."

"No, Mommy."

"Now, Gabe. You can't tear other people's books," I admonished. "We're going to eat food now. Are you hungry?"

He slowly crawled out from under the bed and peeked his head out at me, scowling.

"Nasty carrots?"

"No, it's going to be yummy food."

We sat at the dining room table fit for a large family. The meal was a feast, with platters of roasted meats, steaming vegetables, and fresh loaves of bread filling the table. Gabe was sitting between Ryan, and I. Ryan was feeding Gabe spoonfuls of macaroni and cheese. I was grateful to have a little break from Gabe as I piled my plate with food. On my other side sat Jack, and in front of me was Liam.

As I bit into the juicy delicate piece of steak I had procured for myself, I felt like I was in heaven. It was the most scrumptious meat I've ever tasted. The maid, a short little woman with a halo of white hair, poured a glass of lemonade for me and scurried away into the kitchens before I could thank her.

"How did you end up here? In the human lands?" asked the delta, eying me as I devoured my plate.

"I was supposed to be sent to the Omega Auctions, but I escaped," I said, omitting any mention of the Royal Pack. If they found out the *real* story, my behind would be shipped off to Howl's Edge immediately, considering Jack's loyalty to the Royal Pack.

"Do you think we might send you to the Auctions?" asked Liam, taking a large bite of steak.

"If you're scared of that, there's no need to worry," said Jack. "You can live with my family and meet my sister Jade until you can get on your feet."

"Thank you all for the suggestions, but I'm more than happy here," I said, taking a large sip of my cold and tangy drink.

"Who was going to send you to the Auctions?" asked Jack slowly, turning to look at me. "I can take care of them for you if you know what I mean."

"I don't want to talk about that. It brings back horrible memories," I muttered, taking a big bite of mashed potatoes.

"I don't understand why you were sent to the Auctions. You're clearly beautiful," said Jack, giving me a once-over. My body burned under his gaze. "Any alpha pack would be extremely lucky to have you."

At his words, I felt butterflies in my stomach.

It had been a while since an alpha affected me like that. His stark gaze and honest words didn't hide some ulterior evil motive. But I'd never know. Alphas could be charming one moment and then an asshole the next.

"Yeah...I don't feel like talking about it," I said. "I need to put Gabe down for his nap."

And with that, I was able to escape the intense line of questioning.

Chapter 5

Jack

It was the next morning, and Vanessa still hadn't woken up. I figured she might not be a morning person.

I waited impatiently in the living room, chewing on a blueberry bagel.

"We should be able to take a flight tomorrow morning," I told Liam and Ryan. Liam was slouched on the couch, typing away on his laptop as always, and Ryan was pacing around the living room watching the morning news.

"Do you think the plants will be boxed up and loaded by tomorrow?" Liam asked while furiously typing away on his story.

Deltas were known for constantly working out and being bodyguards for a living. They were coveted by the Royal Pack, but they threw me the *one* delta who loved writing instead. I admired Liam, but he wouldn't come in very useful if we were to fight against another pack. It's one of the reasons I wasn't ready to take on an omega into my pack. I needed at least a couple of other alphas to help keep an omega safe from other neighboring alphas. I needed to grow my pack before I even thought of getting an omega.

"Vanessa is taking forever," I mumbled, sipping my coffee. But I started to hear Gabe crying upstairs. "I need to let her know our flight plans for tomorrow before I oversee our human workers packing the plants."

"Why not just leave her here?" said Ryan. "She clearly built a life for herself. Why do you have to barge in and take over? Or is it your alpha nature?"

"She's one of our own," I said, annoyed that Ryan was entirely on her side. "We protect our own. If I left her here and something happened to her, I would regret it for the rest of my life. Plus, it's our civic duty."

"To the kingdom? Not everything they do is right," said Ryan. "You're way too loyal to them ever since they entrusted you with the Azatine plant."

He was partly right.

The Royal Pack entrusted me with keeping the Azatine plant location a secret. There were multiple locations where the plant was grown, but the supply was limited. It needed careful attention, and there was only one greenhouse on Howl's Edge protected by a strong force of security.

"The kid is still crying," I said, noticing Gabe's cries hadn't stopped. "I'll check on him and see if she's alright."

I stood in front of Vanessa's room door. Gabe's cries were still ongoing, but I couldn't hear Vanessa at all.

Cracking the door open, I saw Gabe standing on the bed, balancing precariously on the edge. Rushing over to him, I lifted him up before he could fall. He continued to freak out on my shoulder, furiously trying to pull away.

"It's okay, buddy," I said. Looking around, I didn't see Vanessa anywhere. I noticed a light coming from beneath her bathroom door.

She must be in there taking a bath.

"He's still crying?" commented Ryan from the door.

"Come here and fucking help out," I said. All of a sudden, Gabe stopped crying and looked at me curiously.

"Oh my god, don't curse in front of a kid," said Ryan like a mother hen. "I'll have the maid cook breakfast for him." Ryan turned and left, and now I was alone with this kid who was staring at me like a stranger.

"Do you like reading books?" I asked, grabbing a nature magazine from the nightstand I left for guests. I instantly saw the pile of crumpled papers scattered underneath the bed that Gabe furiously ripped from one of my favorite books. I tried to piece the shredded papers together but soon gave up. It was my fault for bringing him here anyway.

"I want mommy," he said, sucking his thumb.

"She's just in the bathroom and will be here soon," I comforted him. Then, opening the magazine, I pointed out the various giraffes and animals. "This giraffe is lonely because his neck is longer than everyone else." I was horrible at story-telling, but he was engrossed all the same.

"No friend for giraffe?" asked Gabe.

"Nope, but one day he does," I replied, continuing to make up a random story as we flipped through the pages.

"Time for breakfast," said Ryan, coming in with a plate of scrambled eggs and a waffle covered in syrup.

"Yummy waffles!" said Gabe.

"Good," said Ryan, plopping down onto the floor next to us. I was getting worried about Vanessa. She'd been in there a while without a sound.

"I don't hear anything from the bathroom," I said. "Ryan, watch the kid. I'll check on Vanessa."

Leaving the now-happy Gabe with Ryan, I walked to the bathroom and knocked on the door twice.

Nothing.

I twisted the doorknob, hoping it wasn't locked. It wasn't, thank god.

Peeking in, I saw her outline behind the white shower curtain sitting in the tub, her head slumped to the side.

My heart began beating faster.

"Vanessa?"

I rushed over and flung the curtain open. Her eyes were closed, and her face was pale, with tears streaming down her face. I noticed her ample breasts, her pink nipples round from the cold. I pressed my hand over her left breast and was relieved to feel her breathing. "Wake up, Vanessa." Then, placing a hand on her shoulder, I gently shook her awake.

Vanessa's eyes shot open in panic.

"What? What?" she asked, disoriented, looking down at her naked body in the tub. I let out a sigh of relief. She was alive and okay. "Oh, I must have fallen asleep."

"What's wrong? What were you dreaming about?" I asked, concerned. I wanted to wipe her tears away, but I didn't trust myself to touch her again. My cock was stirring to life at the sight of her like this.

"You know how everyone has that creepy alpha uncle?" she said slowly.

Dread filled my heart. I knew where this was going.

"What happened? Did he touch you?!"

"He did things to me that I can't even say," she sighed, blowing a strand of hair away from her face. "And my aunt despised me for it. She blamed me, actually."

"That fucker," I growled. "I will personally kill him myself when we're back home."

"He's not alive anymore," she said blankly. Her face not displaying a semblance of emotion at his death.

"Good," I said. "Were your aunt and uncle trying to set you up for the Omega Auctions?"

"No," she said and clammed up, looking away. She was hiding something from me, and I was going to find out no matter what. But she looked shaken right now from her nightmares.

"Gabe was crying, so I came up here to check on you," I said, my breath catching in my throat at the sight of her lean naked body under the water. The bubbles from the soap moved past, revealing her luscious breasts. I had to get out of here. I couldn't be here. But I was transfixed by the sight of her.

"I'm sorry," she said apologetically. "I wanted to bathe early and relax before Gabe woke up. But I didn't think I'd fall asleep."

"Hey, it's fine," I said, straightening up.

"Could you pass me the towel?" she asked.

"Of course," I said, turning to the towel rack and grabbing a freshly folded one. When I turned back, my eyes widened. Without any shame, she stood up from the water, fully naked and dripping in water. She rinsed herself off under the shower and turned to me. She reached for the towel, and I handed it to her, our hands brushing against each other. Electricity simmered between us at the touch.

My dick hardened as I watched her.

I remembered the lap dance she gave me. Our first meeting and the fireworks between us.

As she stepped out of the bathtub, she lost her footing, and I lunged forward, wrapping my arms around her warm, slippery body.

"Oh gosh, I'm so clumsy," she breathed, her face inches from mine. Her lips were so close to mine, looking deliciously plump and pink. My nostrils flared at her omega scent hitting me all at once.

All reason went out the door.

I pressed my mouth against hers. Claiming her lips under mine. I heard her mewl ever so slightly as I tasted her lips. Her soft lips parted for me as she kissed me back. Then she suddenly pulled away from me.

Chapter 6

Vanessa

"I'm sorry, I can't do this," I said, my heart racing.

I couldn't get entangled with an alpha who was about to take me home and sell me. There was no way I was going to fall for it and comply.

"I apologize," said Jack, looking regretful. "I just wanted to let you know that we'll be leaving tomorrow morning."

It felt like a boulder dropped in my stomach at the thought.

"To Howl's Edge?"

"Yes."

"I'm not going," I said, walking past him and entering the room to see Ryan playing blocks with Gabe. "Thank you Ryan, for the help."

I ignored Jack's presence until he muttered under his breath and left the room. Then, I walked into the walk-in closet and shut the door as I threw on a simple outfit.

"No problem," Ryan said. "I can help out whenever you want. It beats having to fly planes for hours."

"You're a pilot?" I asked, stepping out of the closet in a low v-neck red shirt and black leggings. I would never think this shaggy-haired blond guy with glasses could fly planes. He only looked to be in his mid-twenties.

"I sure am," he said proudly, his lips turned up in a smile.

"That's pretty impressive," I said. "I ended up becoming a dancer here."

"Hey, dancing takes skill," he said adamantly. He wiggled his shoulders, and I laughed. "You can teach me some of your moves."

"I can try," I said.

"When we return to Howl's Edge, we'll have all the time in the world."

"Why does Jack want to bring me back to Howl's Edge so bad?"

"He believes it's his duty," said Ryan. "It's only for your protection."

"Yeah, but I don't need his protection."

Ryan shrugged. "All I can say is, I'm sorry that's the case. I can see that you clearly don't want to go back."

"I don't. It's such a horrible place," I said as my stomach rumbled with hunger.

"Why don't you go eat breakfast? I can watch Gabe in the meantime."

I watched as Gabe and Ryan high-fived each other after building a tall tower of blocks without it falling over for once.

"If Gabe becomes too much, let me know, okay?" I said. "I'll be back soon."

For some reason, I trusted Ryan.

I wasn't sure if it was because he was a beta and not as aloof as alphas. Or he just gave off the vibes that I could trust him. When I left the room, I was shocked that even Gabe didn't cry at my departure.

The dining room felt big and empty while I sat alone eating scrambled eggs and turkey bacon. The human maid had set it on the table, and I would constantly catch her sneaking looks at me while I ate. I knew she was curious about me.

I quickly shoveled the food down my mouth so I could get the hell out of there. I hated being stared at while I ate.

Didn't she have better things to do?

She had beady judgy eyes, probably wondering what three guys wanted with a woman like me. I wondered if humans ever did the sort of stuff we had to do for survival. My ex-manager mentioned that sometimes humans had orgies, and it was all for fun.

Nothing like when an omega goes into heat.

When an omega went into heat, the knotting from her alphas was needed to keep her sane. It was life or death.

Not that I had anything to worry about. I had a stash of heat suppressant pills I had brought with me before running away from Howl's Edge island.

After breakfast, I decided to look around while Ryan watched Gabe upstairs. As I walked past it, I could hear typing coming from one of the rooms. I noticed that the greenhouse wasn't too far.

I've never been inside a greenhouse before.

As I walked outside, I noticed there weren't any guards or an alarm system. It would be an easy escape if I tried to run away tonight with Gabe. My heart fluttered in my chest as I thought about escaping. I had been contemplating how I'd pull it off but walking around the area and seeing how massive the grounds were, intimidated me slightly.

The greenhouse was huge.

Inside were rows of shelves holding pots of vibrant purple flowers and lush greenery, their leaves reaching up towards the sun shining through the skylights overhead. The air was warm and humid, filled with the sweet scent of the blooming flowers. Water glistened on the leaves, and I could hear a small trickle of water from the irrigation system running throughout the greenhouse. I noticed an acrid scent after the initial sweet scent of the flowers disappeared.

I'd never in my life seen these types of flowers before. As I leaned in closer to one of the crates, my head began to spin, and I gripped the edge of the table for balance. *What was happening to me?* I took a few deep breaths to calm down.

But that only made it worse.

"Get out of there!" shouted a rough voice.

Through hazy eyes, I could see Liam's figure running towards me.

His arms wrapped around me from behind, lifting me into the air. My head bounced on his arm as he rushed out of there with me cradled in his arms.

The fresh, crisp air of the backyard hit my lungs as soon as we got out of that greenhouse.

I took in three deep lifesaving breaths, feeling hyperaware that I was in this hunky man's arms. He looked at me in concern as I gasped for breath.

"What happened in there?" I said hoarsely. "There was no warning sign. Nothing."

"We never expected an omega to go in there," said Liam. "These flowers that make up the component of the heat suppressants are toxic in large quantities specific to your body. You should never have gone in there."

"But you should have warned me that would happen!"

"I admit we should have. I'm sorry about that," said Liam, still inspecting my face for any signs of frailty.

"You can put me down now," I said, my head feeling clearer after getting out of the hellish greenhouse of poison.

"Let me at least bring you into the house," Liam insisted, walking with me towards the house. He looked straight ahead, his eyebrows pulled together in concern, a serious look on his face. His large palms under my knees and elbows warmed every inch of my skin, which my omega self didn't seem to mind.

He brought me into his office and sat me down on a chair.

"Why am I here in your office?" I asked, looking around at the lonely black laptop and a painting of a dolphin behind him.

"I need to make sure you are safe. So I'm keeping an eye on you for a little while," he said, rolling a chair in front of me and sitting backward on it, his legs spread in front of me while resting his chin on the headrest.

"What do you do in here?"

"I'm writing a book," he said, his eyes flicking over to his laptop. A word document was sitting there with blocks of words on the pages. I shuddered. I never did well in school, and it wasn't my thing.

"That's pretty cool," I said.

Wow, a beta pilot and now a delta writer. This pack couldn't get any nerdier, and well...I liked it. It felt like they cared more about the world than most alphas, who only cared about snagging the hottest omega on the market. "What made you decide to be a writer?"

He sighed. "Most people are disappointed when they hear what I do. It's just something I'm drawn to."

"I think it's amazing," I said softly, unable to look away from his eyes and his strong chin.

"Really?" he asked, eyes lighting up. He slid the chair closer to mine until he was directly in front of me.

It felt magnetic.

We stared into each other's eyes, and he leaned forward, tilting my chin with his little finger. Then he kissed me, and against my better judgment, I allowed it. His lips were firm against mine as we kissed. He was the second pack member I kissed in a day.

My omega needs hadn't been met in a long time, only satisfied by a measly human for years.

Liam's sideburns brushed my skin as I wrapped my fingers into his neat hair. His tongue pushed between my lips, tasting me. Our tongues danced around each other, and I had to give him credit. I'd never had such an amazing kiss in my life.

Breathless, I pulled away, and I heard him let out a groan.

"Why not just keep me as an omega?" I asked, wondering why they hadn't decided to claim me. They clearly didn't have an omega in their pack.

"Jack won't be too happy about it," he answered without looking me in the eyes. The swift rejection stung, but I didn't want to seem desperate or beg, so I steered the conversation away.

"So, what are you writing about over there?"

Chapter 7

Liam

"Vanessa wants to join our pack and be our omega," I said, resting on my elbows on the grass outside.

"Oh, does she?" asked Jack, leaning back in his chair as we watched Vanessa, Gabe, and Ryan running wildly for the bright red ball in the backyard. We sat in the backyard, taking in the fresh air and sunset views.

My gaze didn't leave Vanessa's lithe body as she gracefully kicked the ball. She was gorgeous and sensitive despite not wanting to show it.

"She fits in with us," I said, watching Ryan and Jack looking hungrily at her. Ryan was enamored by her and drank every word she said. He was literally her puppy, doing everything she asked. "There's no reason to refuse her from being our omega."

"Do you know how much responsibility an omega is?" countered Jack. "She would need lots of protection, and we would need to support her and any babies she'll give birth to."

"Is she not good enough for you?" I asked.

"Why do you care all of a sudden? You were never this serious about an omega before."

The truth was- I was too wrapped up in my writing, and she blew into my life like a firestorm. Vanessa was everywhere, and I fell prey to her omega magnetic pull.

"We kissed," I said. "It was nothing like I've ever felt before. Her smell. Everything."

"I know what you mean, man," said Jack.

"You kissed her too?" I asked, surprised.

"Right after her bath," said Jack. "My sister would be shocked to death if she knew I finally kissed someone."

"All this time, I thought you were fucking asexual," I joked, punching his arm playfully.

"Ha, very funny," he replied dryly.

We have been good friends since he showed up at the Omega Ball yearly with his sister Jade. I was a bodyguard at the palace then and was assigned to work with Jack on this new secret plant location. I was more than happy to quit my boring guard job, travel frequently, and do what I love.

"I'm guessing your sister still hasn't been matched with a pack yet?"

"No, she hasn't. Her self-confidence is waning even though she makes a damn good nurse," said Jack.

Jade was like my little sister, and I always joked with her at the Omega Ball that she would find her hunky alpha mates one day.

"Well, you might end up lonely for a long time, too, if you're picky," I said while staring at the redheaded beauty in front of us. I wanted Vanessa into our pack. "Do you know anything about Vanessa yet? How she ended up here?"

"No," sighed Jack. "She seemed to have a rough past, from what she told me. And she ran here when she was about to get auctioned off."

"It's odd someone would auction her off," I said. "She intrigues me."

"Don't get obsessed with her," warned Jack. "She's not for us and will never be."

"You never know," I countered.

Chapter 8

Vanessa

That same night, I was quietly packing our clothes while Gabe slept in the bed.

I didn't care if the pack didn't want me. Going back to Howl's Edge tomorrow morning was out of the question for me. It wasn't going to happen, whether the pack liked it or not.

But if the pack was willing to take and protect me...

No, I couldn't go there.

There was no such thing as alphas being good to their omega. They would eventually tire of me and sell me off. It was just how things were. For now, I could run to a different state, get a job and start over. I know I could do it. I've done it before and would do it again.

After zipping up the suitcase, I laid my head against it, exhausted. It wasn't even that late, but I was already tired from running around with Gabe all day, and the greenhouse fumes did something to my brain.

I still didn't feel like myself.

There was a soft knock on the door, and I sat up in alert. Then, I stood up and made my way to the door, opening it.

It was Jack, and he was shuffling his feet, looking a tiny bit nervous. I'd never seen an alpha nervous before, and it somehow made me more comfortable seeing him vulnerable.

"What's going on?" I whispered, gently shutting the door behind me as we stood in the hallway.

"Liam told me you wanted to be our omega," he said. Immediately, butterflies swirled in my stomach, realizing they had talked about me. I wished I'd never opened my big mouth. I had better plans now.

"I changed my mind. It's okay," I said quickly, and his face reddened.

"So you don't want to be part of my pack anymore?"

"Are you offering?"

"I'm just asking," he said.

I swallowed as he gazed at me.

I couldn't think straight when he gave me that certain look, like the one in *Red Light Lounge* during the lap dance. When he gave me that dark sultry gaze, my body instinctively knew he wanted the dark and dirty from me. I hadn't seen that look in a while.

My brain was telling me one thing, but my heart palpitated like crazy as we gravitated toward each other in the darkness of the hallway.

No, no, no. This was a bad idea.

He stepped closer to me until he was right in front of me.

His thick alpha scent washed over my senses, filling my nostrils with his captivating aroma. I wanted him to hold me against his chest one last time and feel his hardness against me. I stood stock still like a frightened rabbit caught unaware by her alpha. I couldn't trick him like this. I had to make him trust me.

I was literally about to run away tonight.

But I didn't stop him as he leaned down and kissed me. I absorbed his scent and essence as our lips mashed against one another, his tongue sliding against mine in a tango. My body warmed and heated, especially between my legs. I wanted him inside me. Deep and knotted.

Damn. He was awakening feelings within me. Feelings I tried to suppress for far too long.

"I want you," I muttered against his lips. His eyes darkened with lust, his eyelashes dark as night. He wrapped his fingers around my arm and led me to the room across from mine.

He shut the door.

"We need to be fast before the kid wakes up," he said, lifting his shirt over his head. I gasped upon seeing how well-built his body was. His shirt hid most of it the entire time, but his abs were there, and his stomach was toned. I reached out a finger and traced down his chest.

"I like it," I said softly.

"I'm glad you do," he growled, pushing me up against the wall and kissing me hard. A quickie sounded so hot right now. Ending with a big knot inside of me. My pussy clenched and throbbed just thinking about it. My omega self wanted it badly.

His large hands explored my breasts over my pajama tank top, and he rubbed his thumb over my hardened nipples causing tremors to shoot through my body. I wanted those thumbs *down there*.

He flicked my tank top down, exposing my breasts in the air.

He cupped my breasts as I quickly rolled my cotton shorts down my legs, not allowing me to pull away. He constantly pawed my body- and as I bent down, I noticed the tent in his gray sweatpants.

I reached out, grabbing ahold of his hardness.

I wasn't shy when I needed something. I rubbed my pussy, and his eyes nearly bugged out, watching me.

"What's wrong, alpha?" I asked, watching him as he paused.

"I've never seen…" he began, staring at my pussy. "This is my first time."

Shocked, I stopped rubbing myself. "Are you a virgin alpha?" It was extremely rare for an omega to come across a virgin alpha. Alphas normally didn't save themselves for anything serious.

He nodded. "May I touch you?"

"Are you sure you want it to be with me?" I asked, knowing I was going to run away that night. I prepared to reach down and pull my shorts back up.

"I do," he said.

"What if you never see me again?"

"Then I'd still love my first time to be with you," he said. "If you're okay with that."

"I'm more than okay with it," I whispered, then he ripped off his sweatpants, flinging them onto his bed.

His hands grasped my waist, and he pulled me to him as he kissed me again on the lips. He kicked my shorts away and cupped my bottom. I felt his hardness grind against me, ready to take me.

"I want you from behind," he said, his fingers finding my pussy. "Your pussy is full of slick."

I throbbed and clenched as he continued to rub me in circles like an expert. Then he pulled his fingers back and held them up to his face. His fingers were wet and glistened under the moonlight.

"Do you like that?" I asked as he licked one of his fingers.

"So sweet," he said. "Taste yourself."

Before I could say anything, he stuffed two fingers into my mouth, almost gagging me.

I grew excited at his freaky side finally coming out. He wasn't shy at all. My mouth full, I sucked on his fingers until he was satisfied.

He spun me around and pushed me down until I was on my hands and knees. I grew wetter and more excited, my breathing coming out harsh. Jack squeezed my butt and kissed the tops of my butt cheeks. Then before I knew it, he spread my legs apart with his foot and knelt between them. Facing forward, I felt his fingers find my pussy again, digging deep into my hole.

"Please, Jack," I begged.

"What is it, Vee?"

"I want your knot," I said. "It's been years since I had one."

"Years, huh? Then why didn't you come back home?" he said, roughly sticking his middle finger deeper inside of me. "You need an alpha to fucking dominate your little pussy. What made you think you could survive without an alpha?"

"I made a mistake," I breathed, enjoying his play.

"You've been a naughty little omega," he said, pulling his finger out and smacking me hard across my butt. I flinched at the sharp pain, which passed momentarily. "It looked like you enjoyed that one a little too much."

"No, I swear," I said, waving my butt seductively to him. I throbbed with need as my core clenched repeatedly. With my head bent down, I could see his dark cock, hard and thick between his legs, ready to penetrate me.

"I'll have to punish you with my dick," he whispered, spreading my thighs farther apart. I felt a draft of air hit my pussy, and I shivered.

"I'm going to fill your empty little hole until you cry with pleasure."
He was a monster in the dark. Something he held back during the day.

And I enjoyed every second of it.

"Yes," I moaned when he teased at my entrance, his thick meat rubbing against my vulva.

"Are you done with the measly human penis? Ready for a real alpha?"

"Yes, Jack," I said, slick dripping down my right thigh.

I groaned when he finally pushed inside of me.

Inch by inch, spreading me wide.

The deliciousness of it nearly made me salivate. I lifted my butt out further while he slid inside me. The girth of his cock was nothing like a human dick. It was wide and thick, filling every inch of my core.

Just the way I dreamt of for a long time.

He leaned behind me, pushing himself farther inside of me.

"Are you okay?" he growled. "You're so tight. It feels so fucking good. Nothing I imagined in my wildest dreams."

"Yes," I gasped. "Fuck me as hard as you want."

And fuck me, he did.

The thrusts were incoming, frequent, and rapid. Sharp hard thrusts, his dick pounding home into me. I closed my eyes and absorbed the pleasure and how full he made me.

Fuck.

Every thrust sent me reeling. Sending me over the edge.

My pussy clenched hard over his dick, squeezing him inside me, and he growled his pleasure into the dark room.

"Do you like it when I'm inside you?"

"Yes," I moaned as his dick rubbed against my G-spot.

"It feels good when you clench your pussy like that."

I clenched again, and I felt the waves of my orgasm crash through my body. Sending me into another realm of pleasure. It lasted for ten seconds, and my head hung limp as he continued to thrust into me.

Then he groaned as he collapsed on top of me, his seed exploding into me. He pulled me down next to him, and I felt his penis expand, filling me up even more. Feeling his knot inside of me was the most perfect feeling in the world. But at the same time, I knew this would be too good to be true. I had to get away before I ended up at the Auctions and went to Howl's Edge with him.

"How was your first time?" I yawned, feeling like friends with benefits at this moment.

"Phenomenal," he muttered into my ear, kissing my jawbone. "You're amazing."

"Thank you," I said, smiling. My heart felt so content being here under the crook of his arm, underneath his heart. To feel his heavy body breathing behind me was something I desperately missed. The power and companionship of an alpha. My heart ached as I thought about leaving him.

But I couldn't trust him. Or his pack.

Chapter 9

Vanessa

Later that night, I walked along the road holding Gabe's hand. It was two a.m., but he was wide awake and refused to be carried. I waited until everyone fell asleep before we snuck out the front door. The pack had no idea I had planned to escape. The hard part was keeping Gabe quiet when leaving the house because he chose that moment to wake up.

We were so far from the actual city I worried we'd never find a bus stop.

The roads were empty at this time of night, and I worried for our safety. I'd see a homeless person sitting huddled in a corner every once in a while or a shady character staring at us. When I finally spotted a bus station, I sighed in relief.

I walked up to the little window with the teller behind it.

"How much is a ticket to Texas?" I asked. I heard about that state from Bruce and his dreams of moving there.

He gave me a toothless smile and pointed to the sign next to the window. Looking at the chart, I saw it would be at least a hundred dollars.

Releasing my suitcase, I reached for my purse, letting go of Gabe's hand.

"Don't go anywhere," I ordered as he squatted on the ground next to me, staring at a beetle on the wall. I dug around in my purse for change and turned to the teller. "Just give me a moment, please." Digging around in my purse, I finally found the wad of twenty-dollar bills squashed at the bottom. Pulling it out, I counted them out and was about to hand it over.

I stopped when I noticed Gabe wasn't around my legs anymore. My heart was racing, and I couldn't see him anywhere around me.

I spun around and saw a long black car driving away.

"Gabe!" I shouted, running to the road. I noticed a badge had fallen to the ground. It looked familiar as I picked it up. It was red and gold with an emblem of a wolf in front of it.

The Royal Pack. And they had taken my son.

I dropped to my knees and screamed, tears rushing down my face.

Jack

Rolling over in bed, I couldn't sleep.

I couldn't stop thinking about the mind-blowing sex with Vanessa. What the hell was the harm in keeping her as my omega? I knew in my heart I could protect her. She was *my* omega, and I felt it in every being in my body. When I envisioned her being with a different alpha, my stomach turned.

After being tortured by my thoughts for a couple of hours, I couldn't wait anymore.

I had to tell her without another minute to lose.

Getting out of bed, I pulled my sweatpants on and walked across the hallway to her room. I knocked on the door. No answer. Maybe she was sleeping now. I could tell her tomorrow anyway.

It was so late. I was losing my fucking mind.

I noticed the door was partly open, so I pushed it open all the way. When I saw the empty bed, my heart nearly stopped.

"Vanessa?"

The room was bare. Her purple suitcase was gone.

No, no, no. Then I remembered her words about never seeing her again. *Fuck!* I slammed a fist down on the nightstand, causing the lamp to fall to the floor.

"Yo, what's up?" asked Liam, dragging his lanky body into the room as he stretched.

"She left! She fucking up and left," I said, my heart racing. Did she usually do this? Have one-night stands and then disappear? Did she think I was going to abandon her in Howl's Edge?

"What?!" said Liam, his eyes opening wide- taking in the empty room. "She couldn't have gone far."

"We need to go find her," I said. "Wake Ryan up, and we're getting the hell out of here."

Liam drove as I looked out the windows at the empty roads like a maniac. I was running on no sleep, but my brain was on alert.

"The bus stop is around here," said Ryan. "I don't see her."

"She has to be here," I said harshly, my eyes peeled and watching for her slim figure to walk around any corner. When I saw her, my heart dropped. She was leaning against a concrete wall, with her face in her hands, clearly crying. "Stop here. She's right there!"

Her suitcase sat abandoned next to her, and she wore a pink sweater with black leggings.

When the car stopped, I jumped out and ran towards her. She looked up, looking shaken and distraught.

"Where's Gabe?" I asked, not seeing the little tyke anywhere. Her eyes were bloodshot as she silently shook her head. Goosebumps covered every inch of my skin. I froze, standing still.

"They took him," she blubbered, unable to hold it in any longer. She collapsed against my chest and loudly sobbed.

"Who took him?" I asked frantically. "We need to find him."

"Gabe!" Ryan started shouting up and down the road.

"No, *they* took him," she said. Her sentences didn't make sense to me as she blabbered about the Royal Pack.

"You mean the *Royal Pack* took him?"

That was impossible.

"Yes," she cried out. "We need to go to Howl's Edge."

"Okay," I said without hesitating. I had to take charge. "Liam, drive us to the plane. Ryan, let's go. Gabe isn't here."

"Thank you," she sighed into my chest, her body limp against mine.

"We'll get you there, baby," I said, rubbing her back as we sat in the back of the car with Ryan and Liam up front. "Why do you think the Royal Pack took Gabe?"

"He's the rightful heir. Their only son," she said, shuddering.

"What?!"

The news took me completely by surprise. I had no idea she was that close to the Royal Pack. She *slept* with the alpha kings...I had no idea how I felt about it.

"That's why I had to leave Howl's Edge," she said, rubbing her tears. "Gabe is probably so scared without me. I'm such a horrible mother."

"How do you know the Royal Pack took him, though? And no, you're not a horrible mother," I said, trying to comfort her as much as possible. I couldn't understand her pain. But I couldn't imagine losing any of my family members.

She pulled out a badge with the emblem of the Royal Pack.

Shock rolled over me when I saw it. She was telling the truth.

Chapter 10

Vanessa

They took my baby.

I could think of nothing else as I sat in the helicopter between Jack and Ryan. The mood was somber, and even Liam wasn't writing as he sat across from us- laptop abandoned under the chair.

"He'll be okay," said Jack, rubbing my cold arm. "The Royal Pack will never hurt their own."

"I deserve this," I said, letting out the longest breath of my life. My heart ached endlessly. This hit me way worse than anything I've ever gone through. I thought about Gabe's little hands clutching me and his slobber all over my face. I already missed his laugh and giggles when I tickled him.

"Don't say that," said Jack harshly. "No one deserves this. Least of all you. You were just trying to create a better life for you and your baby."

"I did something unforgivable," I said shakily. I couldn't hold it in anymore. I had nothing else to lose now, so I might as well be honest. "The Royal Pack was going to auction me off because I helped get their princess kidnapped. Voss kidnapped her and convinced me we'd take over the kingdom."

"So you're wanted for treason..." said Jack slowly, looking at me with raised eyebrows. His face had turned pale, and he shut his eyes tight. "You will need to face the punishment of your crimes, but you don't deserve to have your son taken away from you."

My heart sank seeing the disappointment on Jack's face. *Since when did I care about his opinion?*

Apparently, I did now.

"Damn, why'd you do it?" Liam asked me.

Ryan squeezed my hand in comfort. I had no idea why Ryan was still on my side, even after telling them the whole truth.

"I don't know," I said. There wasn't a reason in the world that could make them change their minds about me. That I wanted to feel powerful because I was made to feel small my entire life.

The rest of the four-hour flight was awkward and quiet. I wondered what was going on with my baby and if he was alright. I knew for a fact he had to be in Howl's Edge.

"Crackers?" asked Ryan, holding out a plate for me. I shook my head, hugging myself tightly. My stomach was in knots, and the pack suddenly lost all respect for me. It was okay. I deserved it all.

"We're touching down now," said Jack, looking out of the little oval-shaped window.

When I stepped out of the helicopter, Jack took my hand.

"We can hide you from the Royal Pack," he said, looking at the guards waiting to check us on the other end of the beach. "We can pretend you're our omega but unregistered."

Liam was directing a few betas on removing the crates of the plant from the helicopter.

"No," I said, firmly shaking my head. "I want them to catch me. That's the only way I can get inside the palace to see my son."

"Don't be stupid," he said, placing a hand on my shoulder and turning me to face him. My chin trembled, and my eyes burned with unshed tears. Goodness knows if I had any tears left after today. "We can protect you from them and look for your son."

"I appreciate it, Jack, but I can't wait that long," I said, pulling away from him and running towards the guards on the shoreline. They immediately took one look at me and produced handcuffs out of nowhere.

"Vanessa!" Jack shouted as I ran towards them.

I was probably making the biggest mistake of my life as I ran toward them.

"What's your name?" one of the guards boomed in my ear as I tried to catch my breath. Normally I didn't get this out of breath so easily, but not dancing for a few days had already taken a toll on my body.

"Vanessa," I answered.

"You are wanted by the Royal Pack for treason."

"Yeah, that's fine. Take me to them," I said. They looked shocked as I held my hands out in front of me, waiting for the handcuffs. The skinnier guard quickly shackled my hands together.

"She's ours," yelled Jack from behind me. I shook my head.

"I'm not," I said quickly. "You can take me."

"I'm sorry, alpha," said one of the guards. "But this omega is wanted for treason. We don't want you to get into trouble or be associated with her."

"I'm coming too," said Jack stubbornly.

"Jack, no," I muttered under my breath. He could ruin everything.

Jack motioned for Ryan and Liam to keep unloading the crates from the helicopter. As we made our way to one of the trucks, Jack tried to comfort me in any way he could.

"Don't worry. I won't let them auction you off, okay?"

"There's no way out of it," I said miserably, staring at the sand below me. The sun was bright on my face, and Howl's Edge was just like how I remembered. It brought a sense of comfort but unease at the same time. I wanted to bask in the sand and the sun. To let an alpha pack take care of me.

To have no worries. No dancing and no bills.

But I had a responsibility now. I had to save my baby in any way I could.

My heart thundered in my chest.

The structure of the palace loomed before me. It had never looked so intimidating before, and I knew I was walking to my doom. I had nothing but resentment for the Royal Pack and the alphas who ran the show.

"You will stay out here," one of the guards told Jack.

"That's not happening," said Jack. "I'm coming in with her."

He squeezed my hand, and I took a deep breath as we walked inside the palace.

"Thank you," I whispered to him, grateful for his support.

Walking into the throne room, I noticed nothing had changed over the years. The decoration and the furniture were still the same. King Armon, the current leader of Howl's Edge, was sitting on his throne, talking to his wife, Queen Ophelia. On her other side sat her second alpha husband. The sight of Ophelia annoyed me. Her feelings towards me hadn't changed by the way she glared at me. As I walked in, the handcuffs on my hands made loud clanking sounds with every step.

"Well, well, well," said King Armon, folding his hands across his lap. He was looking at me like I was a complete stranger. I was annoyed and hurt at the same time. These alphas had slept with me and fucked me in their ruts. Now he was acting like I was nothing but dirt at his feet.

"You took my son," I spat out accusingly. He raised his eyebrows sarcastically, his stupid mustache rising with his smile.

"Well, he's not here," he said. "And you're going straight to the Omega Auctions. A king keeps his word."

"You're lying to me," I hissed, charging towards him, but the guard held me tight by my upper arms. "I need to see him!"

I was shocked at what the queen did next.

"Armon," said Queen Ophelia, rubbing his arm. "Just let her see him, and then you can send her off."

I stood there with bated breath, watching him scratch his mustache. I couldn't believe I had slept with someone like him. Years ago, I wasn't in the right frame of mind. He let out a sigh.

"Five minutes," said King Armon.

"Thank god," said Jack.

It was better than nothing. I nodded quickly. All I wanted was to see my son at this moment. Nothing else mattered.

The servants led me out of the throne room and around the palace as the guards followed close behind me. We walked into a nursery-type room, the walls painted a light green, and toys scattered all over the floor.

"I'll wait out here," said Jack, waiting outside the door.

Then I saw Gabe, and my heart nearly burst in my chest.

He was sitting on a maid's lap, talking to a stuffed toy bear. When he looked up and saw me, his eyes lit up, and a wide smile crossed his face. He looked clean and wore a pair of blue overalls.

"Mommy!" he screamed, running out of her lap and hugging me around my legs. Tears flowed freely down my face as I knelt and kissed him all over his chubby face. I lifted my shackled arms and pulled him in for a hug as long as I could. I never thought I'd see him again. Every moment was precious with him, and I was never more grateful than this brief moment I had with him. "Are you going to jail, Mommy?"

"What do you mean?" I asked, wiping my runny nose with my arm.

"Your hands."

"No, I'm not going to jail, baby," I said quickly. "I was playing a game, and now it's stuck. I'm going to get it taken out, so it's going to be a few days. The nice guards are going to help."

"Don't go."

"It's just for a little while, but I promise I'll come back," I said. "Just be a good boy and be nice to the babysitter, okay?"

"Fine," he said, his nose all scrunched up, and I kissed it. I had to keep it together for him. If I started bawling right now, he would be worried. So I spent the remainder of my few minutes talking to him and kissing him every chance I got until he was annoyed with me.

"Did you eat food?" I asked him.

"Yes, look at my toys," he said, more concentrated on showing off everything to me with his chubby hands.

"Time's up," said the guard. His words made my chest hurt, and I felt physically sick.

"Please take care of him," I begged the nanny. She was a round-faced woman who looked to be in her twenties, with black hair tied into a ponytail. She nodded silently as the guards had to pull me forcibly from the room.

I had to get him back. And I vowed to come back no matter what it took.

Chapter 11

Jack

I kissed Vanessa's cheek as we said our goodbyes at the palace entrance.

"I'll see you at the auction tomorrow," I said and hugged Vanessa. Her demeanor felt like she had lost all hope. Her back was slumped, and her eyes looked hopeless. I could tell she was trying to be strong, but anything I said could trigger her into tears. "Armon said you'd be at the eleven a.m. bid, so I'll be there to ensure you're with a good pack."

"Okay, thank you," she said, her eyes empty and void of excitement. She didn't look at me as she gazed off into the distance, in her thoughts.

"Don't give up, Vee," I said, squeezing her hands in mine. I reached up to push her hair back from her face. It hurt to see her like this. Even after hearing about what she did to the Royal Pack, I felt a connection with her. Maybe because she spent a few days in my house, and we naturally formed a bond. Her scent also called to me like no other.

"I'm trying, Jack," she said, her voice shaky as she glanced at the guards behind us as they glared impatiently at her. "An omega like me doesn't have a chance in Howl's Edge. You know this."

"Vanessa," I said, turning her face. "Look at me."

She swallowed and looked up. "I know what you're going to say, Jack. That everything is going to be alright, blah blah."

"I'm going to be there tomorrow at the auction," I said, looking at her directly in the eyes. "And I will be the one to have you. Do you understand?"

Her eyes flickered, and she slowly licked her lips. "Will you help me get my son back?"

"Everything in my power," I promised. I couldn't let her go weak and broken. She needed hope even though I hadn't a clue how we'd ever get Gabe back. He was royalty, and one of the alphas in there was his father.

She smiled with her full lips, and I let out a heavy breath of relief. I was able to make her smile.

At least for now.

"I'll see you tomorrow then," she said, giving me a quick peck on the lips before disappearing into the car waiting for her. I watched her close the door as she gave me one last wave, and I waved back.

At her departure, a sense of loss entered me. I'd be at the auctions tomorrow and make her my omega forever.

***

Later that evening, my packmates and I sat around the dinner table in my sister's apartment.

"Are you sure about this omega?" asked my sister, Jade, plopping the entire pot of soup on the table. I had dropped the bomb on them that I was thinking of getting Vanessa back.

Who knows what type of horrors she was going through right now?

"I think it's an amazing idea," said Ryan, scooping a ladle into his bowl. "I like her a lot. I know she committed a crime, but she was trying to improve her life."

"How about you, Liam?" I asked. "What do you think?"

He was quietly sipping on the hot soup like it was nothing.

Shit, I already burned the tip of my tongue with the searing soup. He looked deep in thought as he rubbed his small beard.

"She needs a real pack of alphas, as you said," Liam said. "Who's going to help her through her heat? She needs plenty of knots to go around."

Did he have a change of heart after Vanessa's confession? He didn't seem as crazy about her anymore.

"You have a point," I sighed. "But for now, we need to do it and save her from being sold to some random pack."

"I don't know," Liam said warily, but that spark came back to his eyes. I knew he was still obsessed with her, but he was hiding it.

"I think you'll do an amazing job as a pack mate and leader," said my sister Jade, looking at me with admiration. It was her off day from her nursing job, and we usually came over to her place on Thursdays to talk about life or just hang out. She looked similar to me with dark eyes, olive skin tone, and dark hair. She was more on the chubbier side and felt self-conscious about herself around potential alpha packs. "And honestly, she sounds like a really cool girl."

"You'll be an insta-aunt," I said.

"Really?! She has a child too?"

Liam's face saddened. "He's with the Royal Pack now. There's no chance in hell we can ever get him back."

"Man, I miss the kid already," said Ryan, shaking his head sadly and pushing his mop of blond hair away from his face. "It sucks she has to go through this. As a mother."

"I feel for her, bro," said Liam, already finished with the soup.

"The least we could do is offer Vee a safe space," I said. "So tomorrow, we'll be there at eleven a.m. sharp."

"So you've decided on bringing her in?" asked Liam, licking his lips.

I could just imagine all the dirty thoughts he was thinking but wasn't saying in front of my sister. His eyes had a dark, feral look in them, and it was something I felt before I finally fucked her before coming to Howl's Edge.

"Yeah, but I neglected to mention something," I said.

"What is that?" asked Ryan.

"I slept with her already."

"What?!"

Chapter 12

Vanessa

I woke up freezing the next morning.

Stretching on the top bunk, I rubbed my cold feet. The thin, scratchy blanket did nothing to help with the cold. I was sleeping in a place that looked like a freaking warehouse with a bunch of other omegas in bunk beds.

I hated every second of being here.

It reminded me of my past life- before the leaders of Howl's Edge courted me. This was a nightmare on repeat, and like I was living my past life all over again. The giant clock on the wall said 8:30 am.

I was damn well familiar with this place since my uncle tried to sell me numerous times, but I'd sabotage every attempt or run away. All my aunt and uncle saw were dollar signs when I was around them. I was nothing more to them.

Rubbing my eyes, I saw a couple of omegas silently walking around and picking out dresses from the long rack on the other end of the large warehouse. Yawning, I contemplated running away from here, but years ago, security was lax. Everything looked different now. Sure enough, there was an alpha guard at the door, watching our every move with his nostrils flared at our omega scents mingling about.

I climbed down the bunk bed and grabbed the backpack that I still had, which was full of my essentials. The omega on the bottom bunk was still sleeping, wrapped in two thin blankets. *Where the hell did she find another blanket?* I could only see wisps of her hair sticking out from the top.

Locating a bathroom, I washed my face and brushed my teeth, thankful I packed some things.

When I walked out of the bathroom, a bald man was running around and clapping his hands- waking up the rest of the omegas. There were about ten of us in the room today.

"Chop chop! Get ready, ladies. The auction's at nine," he announced, panicking.

What? No, Jack was supposed to be here at eleven.

"It was supposed to be at eleven," I said.

"You're going to the nine o'clock, young lady," he said, rushing over to me and picking at my too-big sweater. He was a beta and smelled strongly of cologne, making my head spin.

"Please let me do the eleven o'clock one," I said. "I'm not feeling well right now."

"Get changed into a dress before our makeup artists get here," he scolded me, completely ignoring my request. Figured. "There's nothing special about you, my dear."

With that, he left the room, and I was forced to sift through the number of hideous dresses on the rack. If Jack came at eleven, I was screwed one hundred percent.

My only hope was that no one would want me.

As I walked with the omegas to the front of the dreary warehouse- I noticed the morning crowd of alphas waiting for our arrival. My heart rate increased, and my palms grew sweaty as I climbed up the steps onto the stage. The sunlight beat down on us, causing several people to shade their faces with their hands.

Once we were on the stage, I listened as the auctioneer began his opening speech:

"Welcome to the Omega Auctions! Where all your mating dreams come true. Here, you will see twelve stunning omegas, ripe for the picking and ready to bear you all the babies you desire."

He began with the first girl down the line, and my heart raced in my chest as I scanned the crowd of alphas shouting out numbers. My eyes stopped on the biggest and tallest alpha there, standing with his arms crossed. He had bright red hair that hung straight down to his shoulders and piercing green eyes. His strong jawline showed off his alpha masculinity and strength. Even the basic blue shirt he wore looked sexy as fuck on him.

He was observing the line of omegas. When his eyes met mine, it was like fate happened. A string of emotions pulled through me, wanting to bond with him. To cuddle into his muscular chest.

I quickly looked down, my heart beating like crazy. I remembered that I wore the ugliest dress I could find. It was a short purple dress that stopped just above my knees with strands of thread hanging off the bottom. To top it off, it was full of glitter on the sleeves that went down to my elbow.

I tried not to make eye contact with any of the alphas after that.

I didn't want to be sold off. Not until Jack got here. I had to make it through this. Before I knew it, the time came when the auctioneer screamed out my name.

He grabbed me by the arm and pulled me to the front with him on the stage. When he spoke into the microphone, I cringed when I saw droplets of his spit flying all over it.

"Here we have Vanessa!" he said, lifting my arm up. "This fiery redheaded beauty is just waiting for an alpha to sink into her. Any takers?"

The bids began rolling in, and I was surprised. In the past, no one wanted a scrawny nineteen-year-old. But, after giving birth, I was more voluptuous, with my boobs not even fitting into the dress I picked.

"$500."

"$1000."

My heart sank as I watched the alphas bid over me. I was going to be sold for sure. I looked everywhere for Jack, but I didn't see any sign of him. None at all. This was it. I didn't see any way out of it.

"$10,000!"

I gasped at the offer and quickly looked to see who roared such an atrocious amount. Even the omegas behind me in line gasped at the huge price increase. It was the redheaded alpha, and he was smirking when the crowd of alphas grew silent. His stark eyes were on me as I looked at him. His gaze lingered on my face in a predatory way, ready to take what was his.

I gulped as my pulse raced.

That was the last and final offer.

"Going once, going twice," shouted the auctioneer. "Sold!"

Fuck it.

My life was completely over now.

Chapter 13

Jack

As I drove to the Omega Auctions, I had a sick foreboding feeling in my stomach. The Omega Auctions were at an obscure location of the island, which I had never gone to. My mind raced with thoughts on how Vanessa must be feeling. What were they putting her through? Was she okay?

Ryan sensed my discomfort, placing a hand on my shoulder as I drove.

"We'll find her and get her out of there," he said. Betas were more sensitive to feelings than us alphas, so I wasn't surprised he could see my tension as I drove, my hands tight on the steering wheel.

"I really hope so," I muttered, squinting my eyes from the bright sun.

Ryan pushed his large glasses up, sighing heavily.

"What's wrong, Ryan?" asked Liam from the backseat, his huge frame taking up two seats.

"I wish we never threatened her that we'd take her to Howl's Edge. None of this would have happened," said Ryan. "She would have kept living a simple human life with her baby."

"We can't think like that," said Liam sharply. "It will send you off into a spiral, and trust me, depression isn't fun."

Liam had gone through a dark time in his life, struggling with wanting to do what he loved and going against society's expectations of him. His family even disowned him.

"We'll get her back and her son. And I don't care what it takes to reunite them," I said, forcing optimism into my voice.

At eleven a.m. sharp, we stood amongst the other alphas at the Omega Auctions.

I felt like a creep standing between their sweaty bodies. The alphas were eager to get a glimpse of the omegas. The Omega Auction wasn't outlawed or banned as it was seen as a humane way to ensure any unwanted omegas matched with an alpha pack. My gaze instantly swiveled to the line of omegas standing in a straight row on the stage. The auctioneer was loud and obnoxious, talking excitedly into the microphone and wearing a fancy suit.

"Where's Vanessa?" asked Liam, shading his eyes.

Chills went through my body. I scanned the whole area just in case, but there was no mistaking it. Vanessa wasn't here.

"Fuck," I whispered to myself.

I barged through the crowd of alphas towards the front. I waved my hands like a crazy person, trying to get the auctioneer's attention.

The auctioneer stopped his speech.

"Someone looks a little too eager," joked the auctioneer, and the audience of alphas laughed. Some of the omegas even looked in my direction, preening themselves.

"Where's Vanessa?!" I shouted. He was standing above me on the stage, and I hoped he could hear me. He clearly did when he suddenly smiled.

My hands balled into fists.

"Where is she, you fucker?" Liam demanded, standing by my side. His fierce delta energy radiated off him, and the auctioneer was no longer smiling as he rubbed his bald head with a napkin.

"She was sold already at the nine o'clock auction," he stated.

Blood boiled through my body as I tried to control my temper.

"To who?"

"The Stoneclaw Pack."

Dread overwhelmed me.

"Thank you, that's all I needed to know," I said, stalking away and quickly heading back toward my car. Vanessa was gone and sold to my worst enemy. I couldn't fucking believe it.

"Do you even know the Stoneclaw Pack?" asked Ryan rushing over to me.

"I do," I muttered darkly. My packmates gathered around me as I tried to clear my thoughts to explain. This was a no-win situation.

"What is it? How do you know these guys?" Liam pressed, breathing hard.

I rubbed my face in frustration as I paced back and forth.

"The Stoneclaw Pack is led by an alpha named Alex," I started. "A redheaded brute of an alpha."

I grew tongue-tied, not wanting to explain further.

"Go on," Ryan prodded.

"We went to the same alpha training classes," I said. "I was the smallest of all of them, and Alex used me as a punching bag for all the fighting sessions. It was the worst time in my life when I was just fourteen years old."

"Is that why you don't have many alpha buddies?" asked Ryan. The question hit me right in the gut. I never trusted packs of alphas or even single alphas altogether. I kept my distance.

"Maybe," I said, shutting my eyes tightly. "We'll never get her back. He has three other alphas in his pack, and we don't stand a chance."

Liam grabbed me by the arm. His fingers dug into my skin until it hurt.

"Don't let your past fears stop you, man," he said. "I can feel your fear and hesitation. Trust me. But you need to go after her. Do you want her to get hurt?"

"No," I burst out at the thought. If anyone maliciously touched a hair on her precious head, they were dead to me. Dead.

"Then?" said Ryan. "Isn't Vanessa your omega?"

"She's mine. She's ours," I said firmly. "Let's start hunting down where they live."

Chapter 14

Vanessa

I haven't been this frightened and uncertain since my teenage years.

I was in a large black limo full of strangers around me. The strangers who bought me. Sitting to my right was the hulking red-headed alpha who sealed the deal with my purchase.

He was the one I couldn't look away from the most. There was something about him that drew me to him.

To my left was a tall, bald alpha with a straight scar on his left cheek. Across from me sat two more alphas. One had bronze skin with a charming smile, and the other was covered in tattoos.

"You look scared," said the bronze-skinned alpha across from me. He gently patted me on the knee, and I felt the alpha energy pouring through him. His calm energy was infectious. My breathing quickened as my omega senses were on alert with all these alphas around me. "We won't hurt you, little omega. I'm Laurent."

I nodded, biting my lip.

The large alpha with the red hair introduced himself next. He stuck his hand out, and I carefully shook it. His hand encased mine like a warm glove.

"I'm Alex, leader of this pack," he said. He then gestured to the bald alpha with the scar. "That's Blade. He's the second-best warrior of this pack beside myself."

Well, he seems cocky.

The tattooed alpha next to Laurent, with dark hair and wearing a silver chain necklace, introduced himself next.

"Nice to meet you, Vanessa. I'm Mason."

"You're a little quiet," said Laurent giving me a bright smile. I wanted to bask in his positivity and joy but couldn't. I was frozen and felt like my life was crashing down all around me. I would have to start a life with these alphas if I couldn't escape them.

"Why did you...purchase me?" I asked, feeling like a piece of talking grocery they had just picked up at a store. I felt uncomfortable just saying the sentence.

Alex turned to look at me with raised eyebrows. As if he was surprised I was questioning him.

"We need babies, and your hips look sturdy enough to bear them," he said simply.

What?! So much for true love and fated mates.

"What if I'm not interested?" I said.

He tilted my chin to face him, locking eyes with me. I shivered as he ran his thumb down my face.

"Don't worry. We'll make *sure* you're interested," he said. "Open your backpack."

Sighing, I grabbed my pack from between my knees and unzipped it. He spotted the bottle of heat suppressant pills and pulled it out.

"What are you doing with that?" I demanded, prepared to snatch it from him. My heart pounded like crazy as I watched him quietly pocket it. Without it, I could go into heat at any time. When an omega went into heat, it was her most fertile time.

"You won't be needing it anymore."

Stepping out of the limo in my hideous sparkly purple dress, I took in the sight of the pack's house. It looked different than most houses I've seen. The house was medium-sized and made of wood in the midst of the palm trees. The ocean shore lay in front of it, so the house sat a few inches above the ground, metal columns holding it up and stairs leading up to the front door.

I stumbled in the sand because of the ridiculous black heels I was made to wear at the auction.

"Are you okay?" asked Laurent, quickly coming to my side and steadying me with a hand on my arm. He held a hand out for my backpack, and I silently handed it over.

"Thank you, Laurent," I said. If I had any chance of survival, I needed to befriend them before they mindlessly rut me during my heat.

"Hey, no problem," he said, his eyes sparkling. He looked down at my heels. "You can take those off if it'll make it easier."

As we walked towards the house, I kicked off my heels and held them in my hands. My feet dug into the warm sand, and it felt like a mini-massage. I planned to keep a low profile when I was around them. To be as obedient as possible so they wouldn't suspect I'd run away.

Just like I had with Jack's pack.

But with every step to the house, my heart longed to be with my child again and hold him in my arms.

The steps up to the house squeaked with every step. I walked behind Alex as we made our way inside.

"This is the living room," said Alex, and I took in the simple furniture. There was a brown sectional, a TV, and a painting with red squiggles above the fireplace. The home was cozy and looked lived in by the men.

"Blade and I prepared a feast to welcome you," said Mason, gesturing to the long dining table full of different foods.

"Wow, that's nice," I said softly, looking at the spread of chicken, vegetables, and potatoes.

"Help me warm up everything, Blade," Mason said, and Blade sighed, the scar on his face looking less intimidating once he was in the kitchen.

"I'll show you the room," said Alex, not cracking a smile. Since I met him, I noticed he hadn't smiled one bit, and I wondered what was wrong with him.

Laurent still held my backpack as we followed Alex down the hallway of the one-story home. He opened the door to the last room, and I noticed the wide bed in the middle covered in light blue sheets. The window was open, and I could see the ocean right outside crashing into the rocks. The curtains waved around from the breeze.

Laurent set my backpack down on the bed, and I wished I had thought to bring my suitcases, but in the moment of getting arrested on the beach, I had to leave all my belongings with Jack. As I looked around the room, I couldn't help but notice Alex's presence right behind me. He was like a hulking beast ready to pounce, and that made my heart pound a little faster. I wasn't certain if it was desire or fear that coursed through my body.

"Whatever you need, we have it," said Alex. I was beginning to wonder who hurt him. Why did he even want to purchase me if he was going to treat me like I didn't have feelings?

"Sounds good," I said, keeping my answer brief. Laurent shuffled his feet, looking awkwardly at both of us as we spoke without looking at each other.

"I'll help Blade and Mason get the food warmed up and ready," Laurent said, escaping out the door and leaving me alone with Alex. I shook my head.

Sighing, I was about to turn and go through my backpack of the little belongings I had brought, but Alex cleared his throat.

"I'd like for you to strip," he said.

Did I hear him correctly?

"What?"

"Take off your clothes, little omega," he said, standing there with his hands on his hips. The large metal buckle of his belt flashed in the sun as he stood before me, demanding to see me naked. My heart was beating wildly, and I began perfuming and releasing my natural omega scent. "I'd like to see what I purchased."

I promised myself to be good. To be the obedient omega.

Even in my dancing career, I never showed my tummy or stripped down all the way.

Hesitantly, I slowly removed my dress, pulling it up over my head. The sparkles got stuck in my hair, and I cursed out loud.

I stood there in my bra and underwear, not wanting to take it all off unless he ordered me to. But he didn't say anything as he walked right in front of me, his eyes glued to my body.

He gazed from my head to my toes, and my face burned as his eyes lingered on the stretch marks on my belly. He lifted a finger and ran it over the stretch marks.

"Have you given birth before?" he asked intrusively.

"Yes," I said. Not elaborating further.

His eyes flashed for a second, then he released me and grunted. "Put your clothes back on and come eat lunch with us."

Then he left the room, and tears stung my eyes. I was angry at myself. I should be happy that he hated my body and my stretch marks. That meant he wouldn't get attached to me. But it still hurt to show myself bare to be dismissed away like that.

I decided I needed a shower.

I felt icky and gross being touched by someone who clearly didn't find me attractive. I was nothing more than an object. I went into the bathroom across the hallway and saw that it was pretty clean. I gingerly stepped into the tub and stood under the lukewarm shower.

My chest tightened as I let the tears fall.

I hadn't been away from Gabe this long, and as I looked down at my belly and at the stretch marks again, I cried even harder as the water washed my tears away.

Later, I was lying in bed covered in sheets, too weak to get up and eat lunch with the pack. I was zapped from my shower cry earlier, and my emotions felt heavy. I wore a pair of red leggings that I packed from my dancing days and a black tank top.

The bed felt too open and exposed. As an omega, I sought comfort from something a little more confined.

Getting up, I entered the walk-in closet and grabbed a heavy blanket from the top shelf. Settling it over the rug, I went back to grab my backpack. In the bottom of the backpack was Jack's shirt, folded neatly. I snagged it before I ran to the bus station with Gabe that night. Even though it was just a one-night stand, I felt a strong connection with him.

Holding the blue shirt to my nose, I could smell his thick cedar scent.

Bringing it with me into the closet and laying on top of the blanket, I closed my eyes, inhaling Jack's scent. It brought me a sense of comfort like I wasn't alone. I didn't have a single thing of Gabe's.

I was all out of tears as I lay there, spent and exhausted. I had never been away from my baby for this long, and it reminded me of the miscarriage I had gone through in my teens. Even before the baby was born, I was attached. The father was my dastardly uncle, but I still wanted someone to love me. Someone who I can love, and the day I lost the baby was worse than anything.

I hoped and wished I would get Gabe back as I laid there in the dark.

Chapter 15

Alex

"Are you sure you're ready to move on with a new omega?" asked Laurent.

"Of course I am," I said, shaking my head and slamming my drink on the kitchen counter. "Why does my pack underestimate me?"

"It's not that," said Laurent. "You're not trusting our new omega. I saw what I saw."

"Mind your business," I said, looking at the untouched food on the dining table. "Why is she taking forever?"

"Probably scared her off already," muttered Blade under his breath.

"I can hear you, jackass."

I swung around the table and sat on the couch in the living room. Looking up at the painting with red squiggles, my chest tightened with pain. My daughter Lisa drew it when she was two. I shook my head, dispelling the bad memory before I sank deep into my damn emotions.

It wasn't the time now.

I had a mission with my new omega. I couldn't wait to plant my seed inside her. To watch her belly swelling with my child, month after month. To kiss her pregnant belly and to feel the baby kicking.

"Score!" shouted Mason and Blade as they watched a game of alpha basketball on the TV. Our team, the Four Claws, were losing but catching up fast. My mind wasn't on the game. I needed to find a way to make our omega more comfortable. Maybe it would help if I was a little kinder. The poor thing was shaking when she stripped before me.

They looked over at me, and I raised my eyebrows in question.

"Go get our girl," said Blade, his tongue as sharp as the curved blade he carried everywhere on his side. "Before I fucking do it. And be nice to her, Alex."

"Why don't you do it?" asked Mason, smirking. "Does the hot little redhead intimidate you?"

"A little," admitted Blade with a wry smile. "Having an omega in the house again feels weird. It's been five years since our last one."

"It has been," I sighed, not wanting to get into it right now. "I'll get her."

Walking to her room, I knocked on the door.

Not hearing an answer, I opened the door and didn't see her anywhere. *Had she fallen asleep?* Looking at the bed, I didn't see her there either. Spotting the half-open closet door, I slowly made my way over there.

Opening the closet door, I heard a bump and a shout- realizing she was lying behind there the entire time. Flicking on the light, I saw her huddled on one of our blankets on the ground, holding a shirt tight against her chest.

Her hair was curled into a tight bun high above her head, showing off her neck. Her sweet scent was heavy in the closet as I took in a deep breath. She was staring at me with watchful eyes. On guard. Like any omega should be when they were in a house full of alphas who could think of nothing but to fuck her.

I sniffed a second scent in the air, and it made my hackles rise.

"Who's shirt is that?" I demanded, ripping the shirt from her hands.

Tears fell down her cheeks as she gazed at me.

The scent was strong, and it reminded me of something from the past. Someone I disliked.

"It's Jack's shirt," she whispered. "Please give it back."

The name rang a bell in my head. Fuck that kid. No matter how many times I beat him up in our teens, the omegas gravitated toward him. Hell, even my own girlfriend from high school was obsessed with him.

"Did he use you and throw you to the auctions?" I asked, gripping the shirt tightly in my hands, wanting to rip it apart and call it a day. But she was visibly shaking and perfuming profusely, her omega scent thick with desperation and sorrow. It was unsettling to me. Something or someone had hurt this beautiful omega. Her strands of hair had come loose around her neck as she sat up on her knees, watching me. I knelt in front of her and gently placed the shirt back in her hands.

"No, Jack would never do that to me," she said adamantly, hiding the shirt behind her like I couldn't get around and grab it again. I hid my smile.

"Did you belong to his pack before? What happened?"

She shut down at my questions. So I decided to try a different approach.

"You said you had a baby once. Where is your baby?"

"I can't talk about it now," she whispered, looking down at the floor. That's when I noticed how puffy her face had gotten and her red eyes from probably crying.

"I had a daughter once," I said, settling down to sit next to her on the floor in her handmade nest.

"You did?" she looked surprised.

"She passed away when she was three," I said, my chest tightening again. I willed myself not to panic. *Stay calm Alex*. I had never spoken out loud about this to any living soul. Not even my own pack. We just didn't talk about it. "Lisa was playing in the ocean, and her mother wasn't watching her. She was busy on her phone, doing her nails. I was at home fixing up the floorboards until I heard her mother screaming outside."

"I'm sorry," said Vanessa, her face crumpling at my pain.

My breathing quickened at the memory. *Don't have a panic attack*. As if she could read my mind, Vanessa laid a calming hand on my shoulder. My eyes burned with unshed tears as I took in a huge breath.

"Our ex-wife couldn't handle that I blamed her internally. I never said it out loud, but I made it clear that I didn't have the same feelings as I had before," I explained.

"That's horrible," she said, leaning her shoulder against mine, resting her head against me. It made me wonder even more what her story was. What brought her to the auctions?

"Will you come eat dinner with us?"

"I don't have much of an appetite," she said.

"I will not let you starve here," I said adamantly. "I'll bring the food here to your nest then."

"Fine, I'll come," she sighed. I helped her stand up, her grip heavy as if she was dragging her body to do it. *Did we somehow obtain a depressed omega? Did she not like it here?*

Chapter 16

Vanessa

The dinner was bland in my mouth as my mind was distracted. I could think of nothing but Gabe. I needed him here with me and safe. It took everything in me to smile at the pack and pretend everything was alright. I glanced at the front door constantly, thinking of how I could escape. When I glanced back at the table, I accidentally locked eyes with Blade sitting across from me. He had a knowing look in his eyes as he winked at me, daring me to escape. His shoulders bulged as he sat shirtless while he ate. All the alphas around me felt like giants compared to me. They were scarfing down the food as I slowly nibbled on it.

I used to have a giant appetite.

Now it felt like hell to chew and swallow every bite. It was a struggle, and my stomach kept twisting in worry for my son.

I couldn't imagine losing my child like what Alex had gone through. It made me see him in a different light. He wasn't just a hulking beast sitting next to me. The alpha had deep intense emotions he had gone through.

"Vanessa, you said you didn't want any more kids when we were riding out here," said Laurent, taking a giant bite of mashed potatoes. "Is there a particular reason why?"

Damn it.

Laurent was the most curious of the pack, always asking me questions. I could tell he wanted to know me on a deeper level, but I couldn't give him that. I wasn't in the space or in the mood to get to know anyone.

"I'm just not ready," I said, staring hard at my chicken rotisserie. Willing him in my mind to stop digging deeper. If they knew where my son was, they'd suspect I'd go after him and stop me from trying.

"It's not like she has a choice," said Alex with a full mouth. "Sooner or later, she'll go into heat."

I smelled the alphas' energies rising, their deep primal scents filling the kitchen at the thought of me in heat. I could sense this as an omega. Omegas usually calmed their alphas down and could tell what type of energy her alpha was emanating. The best feeling was when an alpha would lay against me, fully knotted inside me, sated and content.

But it was different this time.

I still thought of Jack from time to time- wondering if he had abandoned me. That it was too late, and he moved on with a new omega. I didn't think the thought of that would hurt or affect me, but it did.

After we ate, the alphas wanted to play a game of monopoly. Sitting around the board on the floor, I sat between Mason and Alex. I could tell the alphas had their eyes on me at all times. Even when going to the bathroom, someone tried to follow me sneakily. They didn't trust me yet. As Alex rolled the dice, his large arm brushed against mine, and I held my breath as I felt a spark of energy between us intensify. Every brush of the fingers to hand over the dice and money. Every skin-to-skin contact had my pulse racing without me wanting it to happen.

"You're winning," said Alex softly, watching me count the money.

"She's good with her money," said Mason, rubbing my back with his large hand.

"You guys just all suck," I said. They guffawed at my brazen attitude. I was starting to get a little more comfortable around them, but I couldn't allow myself the luxury of just letting them take care of me. And it pained me to no end. The skin contact with the two alphas on either side of me was causing my body to react and get aroused. "I want to walk outside for a few minutes. Get some fresh air."

And also testing the waters.

"Mason will accompany you," said Alex gruffly.

Okay, they didn't trust me. "Of course, not a problem."

Mason

I followed our new cute omega to the door.

"Aren't you going to put on shoes?" I asked, looking at the various slippers on the ground.

"I want to feel the sand in my toes," she said airily, and I smiled. She was such a cute addition to our pack. I loved being around her sweet sugar candy scent, even though her sorrow dampened it. She was lean, and her long legs looked sexy as fuck as she walked ahead of me, breathing in the ocean air. Night had fallen, and no one was outside right now. It was the greatest part of living near the ocean.

Vanessa stood there under the moonlight, staring out at the ocean. Then, to my panic, I saw tears falling from her eyes.

"Are you okay?" I asked, lightly touching her shoulder. I didn't want to scare her off or startle her. But if she knew the crazy thoughts in my head of rutting and breeding her, that would have her screaming far into the palm trees.

Our pack needed another baby.

We had done the healing work and were finally at the stage to mate with a new omega. Blade and I blamed our airheaded ex-omega for Lilly's demise, and Blade fantasized about ending her life with his blade. I knew he was just talking, but we were all depraved in some way.

"Can I have a minute alone?" she whispered.

I hesitated for a second. But realized she was probably coping with being sold to a new pack. I wondered about her past life before she got here.

"Sure, I won't be far," I said, wanting to kiss her cheek. Every fiber of my being wanted to hug her, to make her problems disappear. Walking away, I sat on the sand, a little distance away from her. Feeling a pinch on the back of my shorts, I swore when I saw a crab attached to me. "Fuck off, man."

Standing up, I yanked it off me and threw it into the water. I walked back and forth along the shoreline, watching Vanessa as she sat in our beach chair. Vanessa was staring off into the distance, lost in her thoughts.

I desperately wanted to know her more. To help her.

And her body was banging. The more I stared at her long luscious legs and big breasts of hers, the harder I became. As an alpha, my thoughts naturally went there for an omega that was ours.

Then I passed by our daughter's headstone planted next to the water, and I sobered up. Could Vanessa be going through a similar loss? Walking back towards Vanessa, I noticed she had fallen asleep on the chair, her tears dry on her cheeks.

Carefully, I lifted her into my arms. She was tall, but I towered over her, and I was much bigger. She was light in my arms, her breasts bouncing as I walked her to the house. Thankfully, she didn't wake up. The rest of the pack looked at me as I carried her inside, some of them looking envious. But I didn't care. I had her warm body cuddled in my arms at this moment.

Slowly, I settled her in the bed.

I wanted her to be comfortable, so I decided to undress her. Placing my fingers carefully over the top of her red leggings, I rolled them down over her legs, revealing pale smooth flesh. Dropping it on the floor next to the bed, I admired her fit and shapely thighs as she breathed softly in her sleep.

My cock was hard as I gazed at her body.

Her white panties had a dark wet stain in the middle as she lay there with her legs a few inches apart. I wanted to fucking lick her right there in the middle.

To taste her.

My breathing quickened as I watched her sleep. Placing my hand in my shorts, I squeezed my cock, the crown of it already seeping. I watched her as she turned onto her belly, snoring softly.

I worked my cock, while watching her butt from behind and the dark stain on her panties. I gently spread her feet apart with one hand, causing her thighs to separate even more. As she breathed deeply, her bottom would jiggle a bit, which was barely covered in her underwear. With my other hand, I squeezed my cock from the shaft to the tip.

Faster and faster, with my eyes glued to her panties.

I desperately imagined what she'd look like underneath her little panties. I imagined rutting into her from behind, her knees on the ground. Sinking my thick cock into her tight little pussy. Her warm pussy sucking my cock inside her.

I climaxed in my shorts, sticky semen covering my hands.

Chapter 17

Vanessa

"*You're ours. The omega for the whole pack. To be shared.*"

I was lying in the sand, surrounded by Alex and his pack. Somehow Jack was there too. I was completely naked, ready for every alpha. My breathing grew shallow as Jack placed his mouth over my breasts. Moaning in desire, I wrapped my fingers in his beautiful dark hair. Alex took my other breast in his mouth, and I used my other hand to grasp his wild long red hair. I felt kisses raining down my belly and thighs from the rest of the pack.

And a sizzling wet kiss on the center of my pussy.

Gasping, my eyes shot open, and I realized I had been dreaming the entire time.

I noticed I was in bed, and Mason was lying next to me, snoring while his hand was in his shorts. On my other side was Laurent, who wasn't wearing anything. The room was dark, but I could see the outline of his appendage. And I wasn't disappointed at his size, even during his sleep.

Blade slept on the floor, his weaponry lying next to him, and Alex slept at the edge of the bed. I realized my leggings were on the ground, and my face warmed, remembering I had fallen asleep on the beach. It was probably Mason who had tucked me into bed.

I decided I needed a drink of cold water. I was parched. Especially from the naughty dream I just had.

Slowly and carefully, I navigated out of bed without waking up anyone. I could feel my drenched panties against my privates as I walked to the kitchen. My dream was wild, but being off the heat suppressants made my hormones go crazy.

The house was simple, and I was able to get to the fridge easily. Pulling out a jug of water and setting it on the counter, I rummaged through the cabinets for a cup. They didn't have many dishes, but I was able to find one.

Facing the counter, I downed a full glass of cold water like it was nothing. Maybe my thirst had something to do with my dream. I had no idea. Hearing footsteps behind me, I quickly spun around, seeing Alex appear from the dark. He wore a white shirt with briefs, and his hair tousled messily around his head.

"Thirsty?" he asked, leaning an elbow against the counter.

"You didn't have to get out of bed," I said in a low voice.

"I sleep with one eye open, baby," he said. "I know everything that goes on around here. Why are you awake at this time?"

"I had a nightmare," I said hastily, choking on the water when it went down the wrong pipe. He quickly approached me, patting me on the back until I could regain my bearings. "Ugh, sorry."

"What was the nightmare about?"

"Nothing," I said, setting the glass cup on the counter and turning away from him. If he saw my pink face, he'd know something was up.

"If you don't tell me...."

"Then what?" I challenged, rinsing the cup in the sink. Suddenly I felt his warmth as he pressed up behind me, his wide chest against my back. I turned off the water and dried my hands on the towel.

He pressed his mouth to my ear. "I can smell your little pussy from here. I wonder if I touched it right now, would it be wet?"

"*Fine*, I'll tell you," I said quickly. If he touched me, I wasn't sure how much self-control I'd have around him.

His alpha scent alone was driving me insane.

"Go ahead," he growled in my ear, pinning me against the counter. Not letting me escape. His scent had sharpened, and I knew he was aroused.

"I dreamt I was naked on the beach," I said slowly. "You and your pack surrounded me."

I decided to leave out the part about Jack. Alex hated Jack for some reason, and it made me curious.

"What was I doing?" he asked.

"Your mouth was on my...my breast."

"Like this?" he said, cupping my right breast in his hand underneath my tank top. My harsh breathing intensified when he squeezed my bare breast. I could feel his heart beating fast against my back as he, too, was aroused. He pressed his thumb on my nipple, roughly rubbing in circles. I groaned. His cock pressed between my cheeks, raging. "Did my tongue do this to your big breast?"

"Yes, you were sucking and licking it," I said, unable to think straight. He turned me around and lifted my tank top over my head, revealing my pale boobs.

"So big and juicy," he said, lifting my breasts.

Lifting them to his face.

Slick dampened my panties as he carefully took one of my boobs in his mouth, rolling his wet warm tongue over my nipple while squeezing my other breast. I clenched my thighs together, but he pushed his knee between them.

Keeping my thighs separated.

"Oh," I moaned as he sucked on my breast. He took his time licking my nipple and flicking it with his tongue for a few minutes while my stomach clenched in arousal the entire time. I grasped his thick hard cock, craving his knot. He suddenly released my breasts.

Desperation rushed through me. I didn't want him to stop at all.

"I'm keeping you up," he growled. "Let's go to bed."

"Do we have to?" I asked, breathing hard, feeling empty without his touch.

"Trust me, I would take you right here, right now," he whispered.

"Then what are you waiting for?"

"Until you go into heat."

Shit.

The next morning, I woke up to Blade staring at me. He was leaning on his side, with his elbow propping him up. Freaking out, I covered my face.

"Were you staring at me all morning?" I asked, trying to flatten down my crazy hair.

"Kind of," he muttered. He was the quiet one, and it surprised me to hear him talk sometimes. "You look cute and innocent while you sleep."

"Um...thanks, I guess," I said. The door was open, and I could hear someone in the shower singing. Laurent had such a good singing voice. Deep and melodic. I could listen to him all day.

"Did you sleep well?" asked Blade, his eyes still on me.

I remembered last night's events in the kitchen with Alex, and my face heated up. My middle instantly clenched and tightened, remembering how turned on I was last night. And how we ended things early. The memory of his mouth on my breast had me flustered at this very moment.

I hoped Blade didn't notice how horny I was getting.

"I did," I said. "But I saw you sleeping on the floor. The bed is huge. Why didn't you sleep on here? Am I scaring you off the bed?"

He slowly smiled, and he looked a little surprised I was concerned.

"I want to be able to stay alert," he answered. "To be on my feet if anything happens."

"There are many of you alphas here," I said. "You shouldn't be so stressed out."

"Anyone could take you from us," he finally admitted. "An omega is valuable, and I have to protect you at all costs."

His forehead furrowed, and I slowly traced the lines on his forehead.

"I want you to relax, Blade," I said. "Nothing will happen to me."

The tension lines on his forehead relaxed under my touch, and he touched my arm in turn. His warm hand ran up and down my arm, getting me used to his touch. I liked when he touched me, and I could already feel desire swirl around my belly again. Without my heat suppressants, I was a horny kitten indeed. But I had to make them believe I was trustworthy.

"I don't think I *can* relax," he said. "All my life, I've been on edge and on alert."

"How come?"

"Rough childhood, watching out for myself," he sighed. "But for you, I'll try to tone it down."

Blade leaned toward me, and I didn't flinch or move away. He pulled me towards him and kissed me on the lips.

My eyes closed as I leaned into his kiss.

His lips were warm and firm against mine. His hand moved from my arm to my waist until it stopped at my butt. I wiggled my butt in his strong hand. He squeezed my butt, and I wiggled closer, arching my hips toward him.

He pulled me closer still, deepening the kiss.

I wrapped my leg around him, feeling horny as ever, pent up from last night's wild dream and Alex's teasing. I broke the kiss when I heard footsteps entering the room, and Blade groaned.

Laurent walked into the room wearing only a towel around his waist. His brown skin glistened in the morning sun, a dark patch of hair trailing from his chest to his navel, disappearing under the towel. I grew breathless at the sight.

When he caught me staring, he winked.

"Hmm...started kissing and getting intimate without me?" he inquired.

"Get out of here, man," said Blade, noticing where my eyes went. "I'm trying to have a moment with Vee."

I was touched that he felt comfortable enough to call me that, but it also reminded me of Jack. I shouldn't be feeling comfortable around them. I wasn't going to be here for very long.

Laurent sat next to me, and I could smell his pineapple-scented soap wafting from his skin. He smelled so good. His eyes feasted on me, and I was hyper-aware of my near naked state. I still only wore my tank top and underwear. I needed a shower, especially since I was so wet last night.

"How did you sleep, my sleepyhead omega?" asked Laurent.

"Pretty good," I said, a little breathless between two alphas sitting on either side of me as I laid on my back in the middle of them. The masculine alpha energy in the room signaled their need and dominance of me.

Blade leaned his head down to my thighs, inching close to my underwear. I shyly covered myself with my hand.

"Why are you doing that?" asked Blade.

"I'm not very clean down there," I said in a low voice. "Let me take a shower first."

"That's how I like it," said Blade. "I want a taste of your pussy before you shower. Always."

"Umm, okay then," I said.

I gasped as he ripped my panties to the side and quickly spread my thighs in one lightning move. He licked my center in one lengthwise swipe.

Top to bottom.

"Never block me again," said Blade, his eyes cloudy as he tasted me like I was the most delicious dessert he had ever tasted. My pussy twitched under his tongue, and he slurped up the juices.

"Oh," I said, a moan rolling from my lips as I let my thighs fall open to his taste test of me.

"It's how he rolls," said Laurent, pulling my hand away to give Blade more access.

Laurent's eyes were glued to my sex as Blade licked me thoroughly until I was panting and melting on the bed. Slick ran down my thighs as I arched my hips for more, enjoying how his tongue pressed onto my clitoris. To me, this felt like a guilty pleasure. Like I was leading on the men.

But I couldn't help it. My inner omega wolf wanted every single attention her alphas could give her.

Laurent moved to my face and started kissing my neck, acclimating me to his touch. He blew hot breaths into my ear as his lips moved around my throat. My breathing quickened. My pulse raced with every kiss and every lick.

I grasped Laurent's hair as I shattered all over Blade's thin tongue.

"I miss omega slick," muttered Blade, his voice muffled by my pussy as he lapped up everything. I was shaking and panting, trying to catch my breath. I lay limp as a noodle on the bed as Blade finished up the job and Laurent nibbled on my ear.

"Did you enjoy yourself?" asked Laurent.

"I needed that," I said, still out of breath. Blade wiggled a finger inside of me.

"Soon, we'll be inside your tight little pussy. Two hard cocks at the same time," said Blade, his finger easily sliding in and out from the slick as he pumped his finger inside of me.

"Two inside me...." I muttered, shocked at the prospect. "I wouldn't be surprised if I had a baby tomorrow."

Later that morning, Alex came home carrying a shopping bag.

I was helping Mason flip the last pancake on the stove. For some reason, Mason looked guilty the entire time I was there, and I was starting to wonder if he felt weird removing my clothes after putting me to bed last night.

"Hello little omega," said Alex, giving me a peck on the lips. I kissed him back, making sure I seemed like I was happy to be there.

"What do you have there?" I asked, looking at the shopping bag that he quickly hid behind him.

"It's nothing," he grunted, trying to step around me.

"What is it?"

"Fine, if you must know," he pulled the bag open and lifted a bright pink box. "It's a pregnancy test for you after you go into heat and we rut you."

My heart dropped.

Fuck, he was serious about having a baby.

"Listen, I'm way too old to have another baby. I'm thirty-three," I protested, trying to stop the excited gleam in his eyes. He touched the side of my face, looking into my eyes.

"As long as you can still go into your heats, you're never too old," he said. "I will even take you to a fertility clinic if we have to."

"Why do you want another baby so bad?"

"Every alpha wants to see their omega with child. I'm no different," said Alex, leaning close to me. He rubbed a hand on my belly, his cock evident through his pants. "I want to fill you with my seed and start a family."

Chapter 18

Alex

Vanessa seemed to adjust well into my pack.

As I watched her play monopoly again in the living room with my packmates, a feeling of satisfaction and completion entered me. It had been a couple of days, and she was starting to feel comfortable sleeping next to us in bed. She would hump my knee in her sleep, but I never told her that in the morning. She was getting close to her heat and I could feel it. I also couldn't forget the first night with her on my kitchen counter and how much I wanted to fuck her.

While she rolled on the ground laughing, I stared at the little pink spandex shorts that hugged her ass. She wore Jack's shirt, which hung loose around her. At first, we were all bothered by the scent of another alpha on her, but we had gotten used to it.

It definitely made my hackles rise on the first day.

The only problem was that I didn't enjoy getting too close to her when she was wearing that shirt. She could be doing that on purpose.

"I win!" she shouted, her hands full of fake cash.

The alphas sitting around her chuckled at her infectious laugh. Ever since she joined our pack, the men were fighting less and acted maturely, especially when she was around.

I sat in the dining area, slowly drinking my black coffee and watching them. She was energetic this morning. I was glad that Vanessa looked much happier than she had the first day she arrived here. She hadn't shown any of the usual signs of an omega wanting to escape or running away. She looked content.

Or maybe she was tricking us all.

As I watched her jump up and down, fist-pumping after an hour-long game, I noticed a dark stain on her shorts from the front. Just where her pussy was nestled in. I suddenly came to a realization.

I should have trusted my gut instinct the entire time.

My heart pounding hard, I shot up from my chair and into the living room. Vanessa turned to me, her eyes wide and her face flushed pink.

"You're in heat, aren't you?" I asked her, watching her breathe hard. Like a rabbit caught.

"No, I'm not," she said a little too quickly.

"Take off your shorts. And panties," I ordered. "I'll check you myself."

She swallowed, her eyes darting fearfully between me and the other alphas. There was no way out, and I wasn't going to have mercy on her. As an unmated omega, it was our job to mark her as ours and keep her protected from other rival alphas.

"I'm not in heat," she said defiantly as she bent down and pulled off her shorts roughly. She stood there in her small panties, her long sexy legs bare.

"Panties off, too," I said, my cock stirring underneath my jeans as I watched her slowly remove her panties. The other alphas had long abandoned the chess game, watching her eagerly. Mason's hand was in his shorts. He had no self-control, but there was nothing I could do about it. "Give me your panties."

She quickly straightened her shirt over her privates, but we could all smell her. She had worn the spandex shorts to disguise her heat. Her sweet omega candy scent lingered in the air, thickening each second as the alphas gazed upon her half-naked body. Her big breasts were outlined under the oversized shirt, teasing us. There was no hiding it anymore.

I took the pink panties from her, inspecting them.

A clear film of slick covered the seat of her panties as I turned it over between my fingers. The musky, sweet odor wafted to my nose as I held it to my face. I looked at her very red face.

"I'm not in actual heat," she said, grasping for straws now. "Otherwise, I'd be in pain."

"Laurent, please grab a thermometer," I said. "She's making this difficult for us. I will make sure. Vanessa, on your knees."

"Please," she begged, trying to inch for the door.

"On your hands and knees. Now Vanessa," I ordered with my alpha baritone, using her full name instead of any of the pet names we came up for her. She was hiding things from us, and I was going to get to the bottom of it. She sank to the ground, trembling before me.

Presenting her bottom to me.

I flipped her t-shirt up, revealing her large pale cheeks, which looked like orbs.

Her scent was like a drug as I grasped her ass in my hands. I used my feet to separate her thighs apart until her pink, quivering pussy was on display. Her scent deepened with arousal, filling the air around us.

Damn.

I wasn't sure how much self-control I had at this point. I wanted to bury my fucking rod into that tight hole. To lose myself inside of her.

"Fuck," whispered Blade, watching with wide eyes. Mason was furiously working his dick in his pants.

I stuck my middle finger into her pussy, and her hips jerked up. She was very wet, and her opening felt warm, almost hot. It was the first time I was able to see her pussy, and I wasn't disappointed. Nice and tight.

"She's hot," I said. "Do you see how bright her pussy lips are? That's also a sign of an omega in heat." I gently tugged on her pussy lips on each side, opening her, and she shuddered under my touch.

"She's very sensitive to your touch," observed Blade.

"I paid a lot of attention to sexual health back in school," I said.

"Probably to stare at omega pussies," muttered Vanessa.

I smacked her bottom, and she yelped. "That's enough of your smart mouth. Did you think you could trick us and not let us know when you're in heat? How are you not doubling over in pain?"

"It'll happen soon enough," she said. "I swear it's just the beginning part of it. I'm in pre-heat."

"Here's the thermometer," said Laurent, handing it to me. I quickly snatched it and spread her ass with one hand. I stared at her dark little sphincter, waiting to be penetrated.

"I'm going to take your temperature now," I said, slowly sticking the cold metal tip directly into her anus. Stretching her anus as I placed it inside. She yelped again, and I smacked her across her cheeks as the stick jiggled between her ass. "Stay still. Before I shove it in deeper."

While we waited for the thermometer to beep, all our gazes were on her ass. I could admit I was enraptured by her large ass. I couldn't wait to see what the temperature said and implant my seed deep inside her. I was going to rut her for days to make sure she got pregnant.

Her back was curved, beautifully presenting her ass to me. Begging me to take her. She was getting arrogant and sneaky for my own liking. The little blue thermometer finally let out a long beep.

Laurent spread her ass as I pulled the thermometer out. Her temperature was high.

She was officially in her heat.

Chapter 19

Vanessa

"She's in heat," announced Alex behind me.

Fuck.

I thought I could hide it, but he was one sharp alpha. I had tried to hide any sign of pain from my face and act extra upbeat until I could ride through it. But he noticed. *He knew.*

Before anyone could say anything, I sprinted out of the living room, wearing just a shirt.

"She's gonna escape, man," shouted Laurent as Alex chased me around the kitchen. My belly was on fire, and slick was dripping from my pussy, but I had to escape. I ran down the hallway with Mason just behind me. My chest was tight, and I could barely breathe.

I ran into the bedroom and locked the door behind me.

They were banging at the door now as I ran towards the bedroom window. Thank goodness this was a one-story house. Shouts sounded around the house and outside the door as I shoved the window open. I saw the door slowly crack as someone hurled their body against it. I hurriedly squeezed my body out of the window.

At that moment, the bedroom door crashed down.

I froze momentarily as Alex and I made eye contact.

"We see you, little one," he smirked. "Don't even try."

Running down the beach outside, the sand was hot under my feet. I could hear the alphas' feet pounding behind me in pursuit, and I knew I could no longer run. Streaks of pain flared through my belly as I pressed a hand to it, running.

I looked back for a second as I ran. I saw all four alphas running across the sand already within a foot of me.

When I turned to face forward again, I crashed headlong into someone. I apologized profusely, and the person held me long enough so I could regain my balance.

"I'm sorry," I said again, recognizing a familiar scent. I jerked my head up and cried out in surprise, my hand flying to my mouth.

"I'm sorry I was so late," said Jack, pulling me towards him. "What the fuck is going on here?"

I pulled away, looking back at my pursuers.

The four alphas stood there with smirks on their faces, with Alex at the forefront of them all. Jack immediately placed himself in front of me, shielding me from their gazes.

I noticed Liam and Ryan standing on either side of Jack, their stances in defense mode. Their muscles were tight.

"Return her," demanded Alex. "I lawfully purchased her from the Auction. You have no right or claim on this omega."

"I will pay double what you paid for her," said Jack levelly. I could tell he was trying to reason this out. To make this as non-confrontational as possible. I tried to control my gasping breaths for air to hear Alex's response.

"I refuse the offer," said Alex right out. "She may be rebellious, but my pack and I had grown attached to her already. Now return her to me, little Jack. Don't think I've forgotten all the times you captured the attention of the omegas back in school. And even now, my omega is clinging to you. How embarrassing is this?"

"If you treated her right, she wouldn't have run away from you," said Jack.

"We *have* been treating her right," said Laurent. "She's in heat right now, and if she runs away, she'll get attacked by every alpha in town."

A rush of pain flared through my body again, and I doubled over while they were discussing my fate.

I collapsed onto the hot sand, my head fuzzy. I didn't care what they were saying now.

My heat had worsened after the chase.

My pussy clenched painfully, needing a knot. I needed something thick inside me to keep this debilitating pain away. If I could have thought I could hide this pain, I was dead wrong. This was nothing compared to the brief dizziness and haze of heat I felt this morning upon waking.

"All your money in the world will not buy this omega, rich boy," said Alex. "You. Need. To. Leave. Unless you're challenging me?"

"Yes," said Jack, and I gasped out loud from the pain and his answer.

"Are you sure you're ready to stand up to the big bad bully?" mocked Alex.

"Ryan, stay beside her. Liam, you're my backup," barked Jack. Ryan quickly dropped to his knees beside me, rubbing my back comfortingly. I rested my head against Ryan's chest, trying to get any type of comfort.

"I missed you," said Ryan, hugging me. "And I miss little Gabe too."

"I know, me too," I whispered. It felt nice to finally talk about my baby to someone and not have to be so secretive.

We watched the two alphas circling each other under the hot sun. Alex aggressively threw his sandals off, and Jack did the same. Liam stood just off the side, noticeably avoiding Alex's pack.

"If I win, you leave," said Alex, making the stipulations. "If you win, the only way you'll have her is if you join my pack. Is that a deal?"

Jack paused for a moment. There was no winning for him.

"Fine," said Jack in a low voice.

"Don't do it, Jack!" I shouted. "I'm not worth it!"

He turned to look at me. "Yes, you are. I'll join his pack if I have to."

While Jack was talking to me, Alex quickly swung at Jack, and my mouth opened in warning.

Jack dodged, barely missing the blow.

"Alex is already fighting dirty," muttered Ryan as we watched them throw punches at each other and roundhouse kicks all over the place. I flinched whenever one of them got hit particularly badly.

I didn't hate Alex. He was in the way of me getting to my baby.

"You've been practicing, huh?" growled Alex, blood running down his mouth as he struggled to get up. Jack roared, charging at him again, but Alex quickly held both hands up in surrender.

Thank heavens, I thought. It was over.

"Is that all you can handle?" asked Jack, helping Alex get up from the ground. Alex spat on the sand and held out a hand to shake Jack's.

Jack grasped his hand.

"Welcome to the Stoneclaw Pack," said Alex.

Chapter 20

Jack

I never expected to merge packs.

But I was doing this for Vanessa and only for her. After all of the introductions were over, the Stoneclaw Pack decided to do barbeque that night. Vanessa had chosen to stay in Liam's lap, away from everyone, and refusing to allow anyone to touch her as she curled up in pain.

I was shocked when they told me she was in heat, but I understood why she didn't want to be saddled with another baby when we had a mission to save Gabe and somehow get him back from the Royal Pack. Liam had been protecting her from Alex and his pack. His eyes were dark, and his demeanor in complete protection of his omega.

"Dude, you're overcooking it," Mason shouted at Blade as he quickly removed the grilled meat from the fire onto a large circular plate. Ryan and Laurent were chatting near the bonfire. Alex was in the house tending to his wounds. None of the alphas could be trusted around Vanessa right now, including myself. Since Liam was a delta, he had more control over her arousing scent.

"Looks burnt," I commented, staring at the charred meat on the plate.

"It's fine. We have plenty to make," said Mason, without looking at me.

"Do you have a problem with me or something?" I asked.

He had shaken my hand, welcoming me to the pack, but we hadn't officially gotten to know each other yet. This guy was covered in tattoos from head to toe. Now I understood why Vanessa had run screaming. But I hadn't done anything to Mason at all yet.

"No," said Mason. Then, with the metal tongs in his hand, he looked over at Vanessa. "It bothers me that Vanessa only trusts you and your pack around her. I don't fucking get it."

"She met us first, and we didn't chase her halfway around the island to rut her," I pointed out.

Mason's face cracked into a smile. "You have a point there."

"Hey, we're not competing against each other," I said. "We're a pack now. I'm sure she'll come around, but for now, be patient."

Alex came out of the house, holding a towel to his nose, and washed up.

"You roughed me up pretty good," said Alex, clapping me on the back. "Past differences aside?"

"All forgotten," I said. But in reality, it would take me some time to fully trust him.

"Your beta packmate and Laurent looked to be getting along nicely," said Alex as we saw them quietly talking to Vanessa and Liam. "What's Vanessa's history? Why doesn't she want relief from her heat and to be bred? She is the most stubborn omega."

"She didn't tell you?" I asked, surprised.

"What is it?"

"She has a son named Gabe. He's the son of the Royal Pack, technically the prince," I explained. The Stoneclaw Pack might as well be informed. Vanessa was here, and my pack had merged with theirs. I had finally given in and expanded my pack, complete with an omega. "They took her son and then put her up for auction."

"What the holy fuck?!" raged Alex, his face turning as red as his hair, tied up in a ponytail. He looked down, his gaze remorseful and sad. "And we were out chasing her like wild beasts. No wonder she didn't want kids anymore."

"If she keeps on like this without a knot or some kind of relief, she can die if any complications happen. Never mind the pain she's in right now," I said, my eyes locked on her.

Vanessa had tears running down her face as she clutched her stomach. She was still only wearing my shirt, which I couldn't believe she'd taken. She was attached to me whether she knew it or not. And I was attached to her. It had taken me too long to find her and hunt down where the Stoneclaw Pack lived.

Alex started making his way toward her, and I hastened to follow.

She would get frightened.

Just like I thought, she clutched Liam's arm when she saw us, and Liam growled protectively, throwing an arm around her body.

"I won't come any closer, I promise," said Alex, holding his hands up.

Vanessa sniffled, quietly gazing at us with fearful eyes. I hadn't seen her so broken down. She was the opposite of the confident, sexy dancer I'd first seen. Her omega heat had taken over and made her smaller. The closer I got to her, the more her scent overpowered the air. I wanted to help her.

To rut her just like every alpha in the room.

"Vanessa, let us help you," I said. "Please."

"I can't have another child," she said, her eyes darting between us like a caged bird.

"We will help you get Gabe back," said Alex determinedly.

She gasped. "You told him, Jack?"

"We're in his pack now. You can trust him," I said. "Let us help you through your heat, and then we'll get Gabe back for you."

She looked tired and weak as she studied the sand below her, clutching Liam's arm.

"Do you promise?" she asked. I could tell she was trying to hold on, to resist our alpha knots. Her body craved us, and she would have to give in sooner or later.

"I promise you, Vanessa," announced Alex with fire in his eyes. "We will get *my* son, Gabe, back."

Her face began to relax, and she breathed out a sigh.

"Okay."

"Bring her inside," said Alex. Liam stood up from the chair, cradling her in his arms carefully.

"Please hurry, Liam," she said in a low voice, and he hurried to the house with us following close behind. I wanted to knot her first, to bring her that first relief. I craved it. I didn't give a fuck about the other alphas.

We all crowded into the dark room, bumping heads and bodies.

"I have a bigger place. We can move there," I said, uncomfortable with all seven of us men in this room. Shit, I had never shared an omega with a pack before, let alone with six others.

"We'll just build something bigger," said Alex hastily, dropping his belt to the ground. He had a behemoth of a cock, which sprung free when his pants dropped to the ground.

What the fuck?

"I can take her first," I offered, ripping my jeans and boxers off.

"We'll go with her choice," said Alex.

Liam gently settled her on the large mattress. She looked weak and hurting as she lay there with her knees up. Alex gently pried her legs apart as Liam caressed her breasts. I settled onto the mattress on her other side.

I touched her face, trying to get her attention through the haze.

"Who do you want first?" I asked.

"You," she gasped, looking at me with desperation. Strands of her hair stuck to her face in her perspiration and desperation. "I want your knot, Jack."

"You got it, baby," I said, my chest swelling with adoration for her.

"Fuck," growled Alex, moving away from her center.

I settled between her legs, her opening drenched in slick. Alex held her right leg open, and Ryan held her other leg as she lay there weakly. She groaned in pain, and Laurent gently rubbed her belly. Mason was kissing her neck, and Blade was powering on the air conditioner in the room, positioning it in the room. In just a few minutes, we would all be a sweaty mess on the bed.

There wasn't any time for foreplay. She was in a lot of pain.

"Just go right in," said Alex, as if every word was causing him pain as he kissed her thigh. I could tell how much he wanted to be the first.

But I didn't give a fuck about his feelings right now.

She was the only thing that mattered to me.

I pressed my erect cock around her pussy, using her slick as a lubricant. A moan escaped her lips at my teasing of her entrance. I gently inserted the crown of my dick inside of her, pushing in. Inch by inch. She arched her hips up to meet me as I plunged all the way in.

Her warmth felt so good around me.

It has been so long.

God, I missed this kitten.

"I need you, Jack," she begged, her small hands grabbing my arms in desperation, her body bowed upwards. Her nails dug into my skin as I pumped in and out of her.

"Like this?" I asked, plunging in deep, and she gasped. "And again." I pistoned into her, raising her off the bed.

"Yes!" she screamed. Over and over, I thrust into her sopping-wet pussy. I looked into her eyes as she looked at me. She tried to reach around to finger herself, but I stopped her hand, pinning her to the bed.

"Someone, play with her clit," I ordered. "She shouldn't have to do it."

Ryan scrambled to insert his hand between her legs before anyone else could come in. I looked down where my cock disappeared inside her sweet pussy, and I was turned on even more by the sight. Ryan's fingers circled and strummed her clit until she was panting flat on her back.

In a few moments, she yelled, climaxing around my dick.

Her pussy contracted tight around my aching cock.

My cock squeezed by her walls made it impossible to hold my orgasm in any longer. My dick warmed and heated with every thrust.

Until it was a raging fire. Roaring, I released inside of her.

As every drop of liquid was milked by her pussy, I could barely catch my breath. I laid on top of her, not putting all my weight on her. She was too soft and frail right now. As my knot began to swell, her eyes rolled back in relief. I leaned down, kissing her on her full, lush lips.

"Just what I needed," she sighed quietly, kissing me back. Her warm breath tickled my throat as she kissed my cheek with affection. "I've missed you."

The men sat quietly around us, cocks hard and watching me as I knotted her with her legs spread wide open. She was a vision on the bed, looking satisfied and loved.

"I missed you too, baby," I whispered, allowing the knot to settle inside her. "Let the others take care of you, too, okay? You can trust them."

She slowly nodded.

"We'll get my baby after my heat passes?" she asked. "You weren't lying about that, right?"

"No," I said. I had no idea how we'd get Gabe back, and challenging the Royal Pack with all of their guards wasn't the smartest move. I was at a loss for her, but I needed her to get through this.

Chapter 21

Vanessa

The room smelled like burnt barbeque, alphas, and heavy pheromones.

It wasn't pleasant, but it wasn't horrible, either. When Jack's knot began to release me, I was already starting to feel the pang of emptiness inside my womb.

"I need another knot," I said, trying to rub away the pain in my belly. My heats were terrible, and I hated them.

"No wonder an omega needs more than one alpha," said Jack, winking. "Look at the line of alphas waiting. Cocks out and ready to pin you down one after another."

I blushed, and Alex chuckled, ready to plunge into me next. Mason's hand clutched his penis as he silently watched. Blade was licking my breast now, and Laurent had disappeared from the room.

"I want to wash up real quick," I said, trying to get off the bed. I was literally dripping in Jack's cum.

"No," the men chorused in protest at seeing me move.

Alex ripped his shirt off, throwing it on the ground. He was completely nude, his cock thick and veined with a bush of red hair in his navel.

"You're not going anywhere, little kitten," he growled, holding me down by my waist. His grip was like steel, making it impossible for me to run to the bathroom and get cleaned up. Even though fire swirled around my belly, I felt self-conscious about Jack's stream of liquid seeping down my bottom. Alex's dick was swinging between his legs, ready to enter me. "You're going to get impregnated tonight."

My pulse raced, and my womb clenched. My body loved hearing those words. Even though my brain didn't think it was a good idea.

I spread my legs open wide and circled my clit with my finger. His words made me respond in a primal way to please my alpha. Contractions of pain squeezed my belly again, needing something urgently. There was only so much sex toys could do.

"I'm ready for your knot," I whimpered, ready to be filled again.

"Even though we've only known each other for days, I'm drawn to you," said Alex. "Just know that I care about you."

I quietly pulled him down over me, and my lips locked on his.

"I feel the same way," I said. "I always have since we first locked eyes at the auction."

Admitting that was tough and it meant I was sealing the deal with this pack. My fingers brushed his hairy chest, and I loved the masculine feel of it.

He was all alpha.

"I know you don't want another baby, and I don't want to force you," he said, his voice stern as he looked me in the eyes.

My face heated up, and I bit my lip.

"Alphas don't stay very long with me," I blurted out, tears burning in my eyes. The pain felt fresh, as if it was yesterday. "If I have another baby, who's to say I won't be abandoned or thrown off to the side again?"

"Vanessa," said Alex. "Put a little faith in me. I will not leave you. Not anyone in this pack will, and if they do, they're dead to me."

As I smiled at his words, he kissed me hard on the lips.

* ——— ✦ ——— *

Alex

"Get on your knees, baby," I said. "I want to rut you from behind."

I wanted to see her from behind.

To see her voluptuous ass turned up on display for me. I feasted on her large pale orbs when she rolled over and presented herself to me. I grasped both cheeks, spreading them. Her pussy was trembling and dripping with white liquid from her first fuck of the day. From the front, I could see Blade standing over her head, his cock hanging above her face.

"Do you want something in your mouth, baby?" Blade asked.

Vanessa nodded and eagerly opened her mouth for him. At that exact moment, I speared into her with my hard cock.

I was fucking horny and ready to rut her.

Grasping her butt cheeks, I slammed into her tight hot pussy hole. She needed to be fucked thoroughly.

She gasped and choked on Blade's dick. I could see the look of joy on Blade's face as he enjoyed her choking on him. He grasped her hair, and she took him in deeper in her throat.

When she smiled around the shaft of his cock, I nearly exploded. Leaking pre-cum, I slammed into her again, and she gasped. Her body was going back and forth between us, her naked back shining with sweat from her exertion. I began to rut into her savagely, losing all control.

She was a sexy hot kitten on our bed, ready to be taken by her alphas. And I was going to fucking give it to her. I slammed my cock violently into her pussy, while Blade talked dirty to her.

"Your mouth is so warm and wet," said Blade. "Suck my cock harder, baby. Can you take it?"

She whined around his cock as I thrust harder and harder into her hot pussy.

"Fuck," muttered Mason as he climaxed all over the chair.

"Your large tit is so pretty," said Laurent, playing with one breast and Liam sucking her other breast.

Ryan was playing with her clitoris, making sure she didn't go without her own pleasure.

Vanessa's scent and pheromones drenched the air around us. I squeezed her butt harder as I pounded into her pussy. When she clenched her pussy, she cried out and choked around Blade's dick as Ryan fiercely fingered her clit.

"Fuck, baby," said Blade as he orgasmed straight in her mouth. I could hear her swallowing. "Good girl, drink every last drop."

"Damn," I said, my cock tightening. On the brink of my climax. "Tighten your pussy and milk my dick. I'm going to shoot every last drop of my cum inside you. I'm going to put a baby in you."

She screamed as I gave one final hard thrust, sinking my cock deep inside her. I buried myself in her to the max until I could feel my cock swelling at the base, holding her to me.

Trapping her to take every last drop of my cum. I laid on top of her as she collapsed on the bed, with me on her back.

Blade removed his cock from her mouth, his knot swollen and red. *Poor bloke.*

At least my knot was snug and tight inside her little pussy, where it should be. Vanessa was breathing fast and hard underneath me, trying to catch her breath. I grasped her hand in mine, slowly breathing over her and purring into her neck. My alpha vibrations soothed her quickly as she calmed under me. She turned her head to the side, her messy red hair flopping to the right, baring her neck for me.

"Aren't you going to mark me?" she said uncertainly. My heart thundered in my chest as I stared at her neck. *She was choosing me.*

"Not now, but I will," I said. Her cheeks turned pink, and I felt bad. I had to keep my promise first. I wanted to reunite her with her baby first. I needed her to have full trust in me.

And to not have a shadow of a doubt about me.

<hr />

Vanessa

I was alone in bed with Alex, waiting for his knot to release me.

Jack had left the house with Liam and Ryan to grab things from their packhouse. The rest of the alphas were scattered, and I had no idea where they disappeared to. It felt so good laying here with Alex deep inside me, his warm body covering mine from behind. His knot inside me relieved a lot of the pain from my heat, giving me exactly what I needed.

At the same time, I felt slightly hurt that he wasn't ready to mark me as his.

"When will that happen?" I asked.

"When the time is right and when you're ready for me, baby," he said, rubbing circles on my back as I lay on my stomach. He lightly bit my earlobe, and I yelped. "And you won't have any regrets when that day comes."

"I miss my baby," I sighed.

I couldn't fully enjoy myself and be happy knowing that each day Gabe was at the palace. Were they treating him right? Feeding him properly? A sense of urgency grew in my stomach. Alex seemed to sense it, and he immediately started to purr into my ear again, calming my anxiety.

"I can't wait to meet the little guy," said Alex, pushing himself further into me as the knot began to loosen.

"He has curly blond hair and the most beautiful blue eyes," I said. "I miss his sloppy kisses and his smell."

"Gabe sounds like he might break a few omegas' hearts in the future," chuckled Alex. "Don't worry. We'll get him back as soon as your heat is over."

"I can handle myself. Please get him," I said. "You can leave an alpha or two with me here. Or you all can go and get him."

I tried to turn my body around to see him. His eyebrows were pressed together.

"I would need to talk to Jack. To figure out the best course of action," said Alex. "We can't simply wage war on the Royal Pack. You have seven males, but we are not enough to bring down all their guards to crash in and save your baby. Gabe is also their prince."

My face crumpled, and I sighed. "I know."

He pressed his hand against the side of my face.

"One way or another, we will find a way. I don't want my omega worrying, okay?"

"I'll try not to."

"He's their son. They'll take care of him."

I nodded, not trusting myself to speak. My eyes were beginning to well with tears, and my emotions were heightened tremendously with my heat. Alex silently hugged me from behind, kissing and purring against me.

Later that day, the alphas came back into the room after I had taken a nap.

"Wake up, honey," said Laurent, kissing me on the cheek. Stirring awake, I noticed it was dark outside already, and Alex was snoring beside me. The room was dark and cozy. I wiggled out from the warm nest under his arm and blearily gazed at him.

"I'm so tired," I said, feeling a pang of the heat circle around my waist.

Alex was starting to stir, yawning loudly, which sounded more like a roar.

"Sorry," he muttered when he saw me staring wide-eyed at him.

"We have a surprise for you," said Laurent. "But we need to get you out to the van."

Chapter 22

Vanessa

"But I want to take a shower first!" I protested as Laurent picked me up from the bed.

"No time for that," he said. "You're in heat, honey."

"What's happening?" asked Alex, throwing his shirt and pants back on.

"We're ready outside," announced Mason, his eyes lit up. "You'll know soon enough, Alex."

"I'm literally only wearing an oversized t-shirt of Jack's," I muttered, giving up and leaning into Laurent's strong arms. He gave me a peck on the forehead after I stopped resisting him.

"Good girl, just settle down," he said, walking out the front door with me still in his arms. I was being carried like a baby, but it's not like I could walk much while in heat. It was too painful.

Blade was driving, and Mason settled into the passenger seat. I sat between Laurent and Alex in the back. It was weird being in a van without pants or underwear on. I tried combing my hair with my fingers but soon gave up. I hoped we weren't doing anything fancy. But if we were, I would never forgive these alphas for not warning me. I looked like a hot mess.

"Where's Jack?" I asked.

"We fought him and his pack. They're gone now, thank god," said Mason.

My heart dropped. I opened my mouth to start screaming at them.

"He's lying," sighed Laurent before I could explode.

"I hope so," I said. Mason was chuckling as he drove. "It's not funny, Mason."

"It's cute to see you riled up," he said, his eyes on the rearview mirror, watching me.

"Pay attention to the road," I said, rolling my eyes. Alex laid a hand on my thigh, comforting my frazzled self.

***

"It's us," called Mason, knocking on the door of the hotel room.

I was pleasantly surprised they had taken me to the best four-star hotel in Howl's Edge. Jack swung the door open, a huge beaming smile on his face. He pulled me in for a hug. He had on a white robe, and he smelled fresh as can be.

"I got us an Alpha-Suite room," he declared. "Do you like your heat gift?"

I didn't know heat gifts were a thing until now.

As I walked in, I admired the wide expanse of the bed in the middle with fresh, clean sheets and the giant living room with a kitchen. I had never been to a hotel like this before. Even when I was in the Royal Pack, we hadn't gone out during the short time I was with them. The rug was soft under my toes, and there was a long sofa fit for a large pack.

I looked back at Alex, and I caught the slight twitching of his jaw. *Oh, he looked annoyed by Jack taking charge like this.*

"I love it," I said, kissing Jack.

Jack smiled and led me toward the large bathroom. The walls were blindingly white, as well as the tile floors. I felt self-conscious as I stepped inside. I gasped when I saw the enormous wall-to-wall tub covered in bubbly water with Ryan and Liam sitting inside.

"Join us," said Liam, smiling.

"Hell, yes!" I said, removing my shirt and getting naked. I stepped into the bath, allowing the warm bubbly water to coat my shoulders as I sank inside between Liam and Ryan.

"I'll get our queen some grapes or whatever fruit we have here," said Jack.

I moaned, closing my eyes. Jack chuckled at my response.

"We might as well join, too," said Alex, stripping off his clothes. Mason sat in there naked in all his tattoo glory. He sat across from me, his feet touching mine. It was a giant hot tub fitting all of us.

Alex leaned back against the tub, resting his arms on the walls.

"Shouldn't we take up Jack's offer on the bigger house?" asked Mason. "I mean, we need the extra space for our omega. Look how she's relaxing over there."

The water was indeed easing my cramps, but I was still very horny. It was a regular side-effect from a heat that didn't allow an omega to see things clearly except for needing a knot.

I didn't mind the horny part. I just hated the painful aspect of it.

I moved over and sat on Liam's lap, my favorite spot today. Except he was naked this time, and I could feel his heart pumping like crazy against my bare back.

"What are you doing, my frisky omega?" he asked, his voice hoarse. "I don't have a knot." Deltas weren't able to knot like alphas or sigmas. Their job was to usually guard the pack and not focus on procreating.

"I don't care," I said, wiggling on his lap. His hardness pressed against my bottom without much effort on my part.

"Give it to her, man," said Laurent, sinking into the water next.

"Not in the water," said Liam. "How will you stay lubricated?"

"I'm in heat," I said, rolling my eyes. "I'm constantly wet down there."

I turned around to face him, grinding against his cock.

"Vee," he groaned as I continued grinding my pussy against him. I wrapped my legs around his waist.

I felt someone press against my back. Turning, I saw Mason as he grasped my ass cheeks.

"I'm going to give you a little pleasure from behind," he whispered in my ear, his little finger rubbing my sphincter in circles. "Is that okay, little omega?"

"Yes," I breathed.

Liam positioned his cock to align my pussy. I slowly sat on top of it, allowing his thickness to glide inside me. Mason's finger rubbed around and around my anus as I rode Liam.

Liam's hands gripped my hips, guiding me as I bounced on his cock. The thickness of his cock made up for the lack of a knot, stretching my pussy to the point that it was hard for me to ride him.

"No more," said Liam, noticing my struggle. "Let me take the lead here, baby."

He removed his glasses and set them on a little shelf behind him.

He then lifted my body by my hips. Pressing me up and down on his cock. I felt like a little toy as he lifted me up and down, pushing himself deeper into me with each stroke. I held onto his shoulders for dear life as he rammed into my tight pussy with no mercy.

His green eyes were dark with lust. Feral and heavy.

The finger in my bottom slid inside me as Liam took me. I gasped. Liam bounced me savagely onto his thick dick, his hair wild around his face and no longer neatly slicked back.

"Your anus is clenching around my finger," Mason whispered. His breath was hot in my ear. His finger was probing well inside my ass. "I love your ass."

I clenched at his words, nearly about to cum- but I couldn't. I needed someone to touch my clit.

"Ryan," I gasped.

"Yes, honey?!" he said, coming to my side. "Is this too much? Should I call them off?"

"No," I screamed over the bucking bull. That was the last thing I wanted. "Please rub my clit. I can't let go of him, or else I'll fall in the water."

"Of course," said Ryan, sliding his wet finger between Liam's raging dick and my pussy. When he started to flick my clit the way I liked it, I licked my lips in anticipation. Fire swirled in my belly and into my pussy, as I absorbed the sensation of multiple males touching my body.

My breasts bounced repeatedly as Liam lifted and dropped me onto his cock. His eyes were fierce on my breasts.

"I like watching your big boobs bounce while I fuck you," said Liam. "Are you scared, love?"

"No," I gasped, dreaming of being taken like this for a long while. Even when I lived in the human lands, I felt deprived of this type of sex that every omega deserved. The thick cock inside my pussy stilled. Liam let out a low gasp as he climaxed deep inside me.

I felt a second finger press into my asshole, stretching me.

"Make her come," said Liam. "I want her pussy to squeeze the fuck out of my cock."

"I have to prepare your little ass for our pack. We need all your holes," said Mason, wiggling both fingers inside me. Ryan's thumb pressed around my clit, and I screamed as I came around their fingers. I even felt a bit of slick seep down my anus.

I let my head fall on Liam's shoulder, and he patted my hair down, brushing it away from my face with his wet hands.

"Good girl," said Liam.

Mason removed his fingers from my behind, and Ryan did the same with my throbbing clit. It was so much stimulation that resulted in my powerful orgasm.

"Damn," said Blade, breathing hard as I heard him have his own orgasm behind me. "That was fucking hot."

Jack stood there with a fruit bowl, naked outside the tub with a hard-on.

"Sorry, I didn't want to interrupt," he said as I tried to catch my breath.

Jack came inside the tub and fed me a grape.

"Mhm," I said as the cold juicy grape burst into my mouth. He fed me a strawberry next as Liam rubbed my back. Mason was massaging my bottom under the water, his finger dangerously close to my anus again.

After our fun in the tub, I was taking a shower together with Mason and Laurent. I couldn't keep my hands off them, and Mason couldn't stop touching my bottom as I washed my hair under the water. It felt good to get clean after my messy heat with the pack. Laurent was scrubbing my breasts with the large purple loofah in his hand, gazing at and adoring my body.

"You're beautiful and curvy in all the right places," said Laurent, rubbing the loofah over my stretch marks. "Exactly my type of omega."

He then dropped the loofah and rubbed my stomach with his bare hands, igniting my skin.

Mason was behind me, washing my bottom with a second loofah.

"I like your body too," I said, admiring how Laurent's muscles bunched around his shoulders as he knelt on the shower floor, eye level with my pussy. The water from the shower sprayed all over us, ample enough water to cover two giant alphas inside with me behind a glass door. From the corner of my eye, I could see Alex sitting on the large chair in his white robe, which was open in the front, watching us intently.

My heart pumped faster in my chest. Having him watch me get screwed by two alphas was turning me on like nothing else.

Laurent prodded my thighs open, and I quickly spread them as I watched Alex slowly grasp his long hard dick. Laurent kissed my pussy, and I grasped his shoulders to keep from falling.

Then he kissed the inside of my pussy, and I felt my slick start seeping down my legs. I was unendingly horny around this pack; they were all muscular and sturdy.

"I love how your pussy tastes," said Laurent, furiously licking the slick he caused me to release. "So sweet."

I didn't realize what Mason was doing behind me until I felt his tongue slide across my anus. Both alphas were kneeling on either side of me, with me sandwiched in the middle- my legs spread as they feasted on me.

A tongue in my pussy and one in my ass.

"Delicious," groaned Mason as he licked me up and down until slick shot out from my anus. I felt immense and guilty pleasure to be loved like this. I tried to clench my thighs when the tongues invaded my holes. Laurent's tongue pressed deep inside my pussy, stretching me out. My anus was being stretched slowly as Mason pressed his tongue against it, straining to get inside.

As I tried to close my legs, Laurent held my legs farther apart, and I quickly leaned forward against his head for balance. I watched Alex rub his cock up and down as he watched me get invaded and probed with their tongues. I shuddered in pleasure as Laurent swirled his tongue inside my pussy, finding more sensitive areas.

Mason's tongue slithered like a snake into my ass, and I yelped.

"Your tongue is big!"

His chuckle was muffled against my butt as he sank it in deeper, stretching me further. Laurent's tongue swiped against my clit, and then he suctioned my slick like a vacuum.

Through the glass, Alex was yanking on his dick harder and faster.

I screamed and shuddered as I saw fireworks when he did that. My legs trembled as they cleaned up my slick with their tongue.

"That was a good feast," said Laurent, patting my thighs.

I saw Alex collapse against the chair, his cock swollen and purple.

"Tasty butt," Mason sighed as he removed his tongue from me. I felt sore, and my holes fully stretched after their tongue assault. But I was more relaxed than I had been in a very long time.

Chapter 23

Vanessa

After a couple of days in the hotel and having sex with every male in the room, I was exhausted when my heat finally broke.

It was a constant desire to get knotted and fucked thoroughly throughout my heat haze. The guys would even take turns feeding me while an alpha would fuck me repeatedly or if I was waiting for a knot to go down.

This morning, I was getting ready to leave the hotel with the men. We decided to check out Jack's spare house that he was offering. Alex finally caved in and admitted that we needed a bigger space now that there were eight of us. I was happy to see Jack and Alex getting along and talking about the Azatine plant business together.

The pack was getting increasingly closer and attached to me as the days progressed. They expressed it in physical affection and trusted me with their personal stories. I was growing in emotional connection with each of them. Jack had taken the liberty of making sure I was fed and hydrated constantly. Alex was rough, but his knot took me to new heights.

Ryan made sure I was okay mentally and physically. Making sure things didn't go too far. Even though Ryan was a beta, he was over-protective of me, which made my heart swell when he was around me. Laurent stimulated me with his wild stories from his past and his love of traveling the world. Alphas, unlike omegas or betas, were allowed to travel outside of Howl's Edge whenever they wanted.

"Are you ready, baby?" asked Mason, watching me put on mascara. Blade had bought me clothes and makeup while I was on my back for two days.

"Yes, almost," I said. "Blade, you got me a size too small. My boobs aren't fitting in this shirt."

The red shirt clung tight against my breasts, showing off my entire cleavage. Blade hugged me from behind, cupping my breasts in his hands.

"That's my bad," he mumbled against my ear. "But I love the feel of your breasts in my hand." I started to feel the familiar tingly warm sensation creeping down my belly.

"You're going to trigger my heat again," I said, trying to shake him off, but he grasped me tight, squeezing my breasts roughly.

"Not unless we bred you correctly," he said. "If you're pregnant, you shouldn't go into heat again."

Worry set in my belly.

The thought of pregnancy still frightened me. I didn't have Gabe at my side yet, but the men had promised me they'd devise a plan. This was the first morning where I wasn't curled up in pain, so I expected something from them today at some point. Sometimes I felt like I was whining too much. I knew it was a crazy thought since it was my baby. But my deep insecurity and intrusive thoughts plagued me late at night when I thought about my baby. I didn't want to constantly talk about Gabe and wanted to give my full attention to the men during my heat.

But now that my heat was over, it was time to get my baby back.

We stood in front of Jack's second house. I was shocked at how big it was.

It was even bigger than his house back in the human lands. A woman answered the front door. She had similar features to Jack. She had an olive skin tone, dark eyes lined with eyeliner, and long black hair. She was a beautiful omega, radiating elegance in the way she moved.

"Vanessa, meet my sister, Jade," said Jack smiling.

I smiled politely, shaking her hand.

"It's nice to meet the omega who finally captures my brother's heart," laughed Jade. "I'm so glad to meet you."

"It's nice to meet you too," I said, hating how stiff I sounded. Honestly, my mind was entirely focused on getting Gabe back and not wasting time with pleasantries. But I took a deep breath and entered the home.

"I'm not gonna lie. This place is huge," said Alex, clapping Jack on the shoulder.

"We can stay here until we can decide on something more permanent," said Jack. "There are thirteen rooms, so we won't crowd Vanessa in just one room. Unless she wants it, of course."

When we entered the house, Jade showed me around the kitchen.

"Sometimes, we need a break from all the testosterone," said Jade. The kitchen was spacious, with granite countertops and a modern sink.

Mason let out a whoop as he looked out the large front window.

"You have speedboats?" he asked.

"Yeah, do you want to try it out?" asked Jack, and I could see them all smiling ear to ear.

But Alex looked over at me.

"Don't worry about me," I said. "We'll have some girl talk while you guys explore."

Liam walked over to me and kissed me on the lips.

"Don't have too much fun while we're gone," he said. The rest of the pack kissed me before disappearing from the house. I could hear their excited exclamations as they got to the speedboats.

"Men," muttered Jade. "How in the world did you snag seven of them?"

"I...it all just came together," I said lamely, watching her chop up a head of lettuce on a brown cutting board. Her rings flashed from the sunlight as she held the knife carefully between her fingers. "Do you need help with anything?"

"No thanks, hun," she said. "It's just salad. Goodness knows I have to start watching my weight." She patted her chubby belly and sighed.

"You're not that big at all," I said, but my mind was elsewhere. We heard the roar of the speedboat engine disappear.

My heart began racing with the possibility of escaping to the Royal Palace. This was the first time I was without an alpha standing guard over me.

I had to see my son.

The alphas were taking their time to come to a decision. As I listened to Jade talk about her work and the alpha she was crushing on, I contemplated how I'd leave. "I'm sorry, but do you have scent blockers?"

"Isn't the alpha mark enough to keep predators away?" she asked.

"No, I forgot about that," I lied. I wanted to hide my identity as an omega so I could take a damn taxi without any issues.

I had to pass for a beta, at least. Betas didn't have a distinct scent as omegas did. My heart thundered so loud in my chest that I could barely hear what Jade was saying over the racket in my brain. The little voice was telling me to get my child, and the other voice demanded I stay put and wait for my pack for extra protection.

"Why do you need the scent blockers?"

I was jolted out of my thoughts.

"Nothing, I just wanted to take a walk outside without the pack around me constantly," I said.

I could tell Jade was starting to feel bad for me, judging by the way she was twisting her fingers together anxiously. After everything that happened to me, I told myself I wouldn't manipulate or lie to people anymore, but I had to do this for my son.

"Well, if that's the case," she said, walking over to her brown purse on the counter after drying her hands. "Here you go. I bet seven males could be a *lot* for one omega and you need a break."

"Thank you so much, Jade."

I took the bottle of cream from her and headed off to a random room in the huge house and locked the door.

This room was an office. Chestnut table and a large portrait of an alpha werewolf. A mini flag of Howl's Edge island sat on the desk, striped in yellow and green with a wolf's eye in the middle.

I quickly stripped off my red shirt and my black shorts. I slathered on the cream, trying not to use too much and finish her supply. After covering myself in the cream and throwing my clothes back on, I was glad my scent wasn't as obvious anymore. Unless an alpha decided to come really close to me, I was safe.

My legs were shaky, and I was light-headed as I exited the taxi.

"Thank you," I called to the driver, shutting the door.

He zoomed away as fast as possible, as if I was an inconvenience. He didn't even talk through the whole ride. *Whatever.* That wasn't any of my concerns right now.

I was facing the back of the palace, where the massive graveyard was.

It was the only way I could enter without running into the guards at the front. After living here for a few months, I knew this was the least guarded area. It was where Voss and I had made plans for our life together every night without getting caught. I wasn't attached to him at all. He was just a way out and a way to my freedom. A pawn in the game on my path to freedom. Until everything went wrong.

As I walked between the wall of trees that blocked off the graveyard, my heart started racing again at the sight of the extravagant building. The divide between the wealthy and the poor always made me question if we were living in the island paradise that we all thought we were living.

Immediately, I saw Gabe playing with Queen Ophelia out on the terrace.

Ophelia had on a white straw hat and laughed as Gabe chased a butterfly off a rose. She looked much older than the last time I saw her. But I didn't care about her. My eyes were only on my son right now. He wore the same blue overalls they had him wear before, and his chubby cheeks were pink from his large smile. My heart ached. I wanted to run around this bush I was kneeling behind and go to him.

To call out his name. To hug him.

But instead, I knelt there, watching him play for a while. Ophelia was distracted and looking at herself in a handheld mirror, her hand covered in long white gloves. I looked back toward Gabe and saw him running dangerously close to the pond. Panicking, I looked back at Ophelia and saw her staring at him wide-eyed. Frozen in her seat.

"Gabe, get back here!" she shouted.

I wasn't wasting any time. I knew how fast my baby was.

Running out of the cover of the trees and the bush, I chased after my toddler, who had beelined towards the pond. He was laughing maniacally, swinging his arms in the air.

"Gabe!" I shouted, and he stopped in his tracks. He curiously turned around and gave me a wide toothy grin upon seeing me.

"Mommy?" he said.

I caught up to him and pulled him close to me. I didn't say a word as I hugged him tight, trying to catch my breath.

"I missed you so so much, baby," I said, kissing him all over his little face.

"You're not allowed to be here," said Ophelia's voice from behind. *Damn it to hell.*

Chapter 24

Jack

It was a beautiful day out at the water.

"This boat is so fucking awesome," said Blade as I zoomed across the water with the speedboat. The wind on my face was the best feeling.

We were making our way back to the dock when I saw Jade waving her hands frantically.

"Wonder what's wrong," I muttered.

"She's acting like the house is on fire," said Ryan. "Don't worry too much, guys. She's always been dramatic."

My sister wanted to major in drama until my parents encouraged her to be something more as an omega. My parents advocated for omega rights and ensured she had the perfect education to get into the nursing program, even though she wasn't as excited about it. She did it to make them happy.

But w̲hy wasn't Vanessa with her?

"What's wrong, sister?" I asked, jumping off the boat as soon as we moored the boat.

The rest of my pack members also joined me standing around Jade. Waiting for her to speak.

"It's Vanessa. She's gone," said Jade, in a panic. Her eyes were wide, and she was trying to catch her breath. "She said she was going for a walk, but I couldn't find her. It's been an hour already."

Panic shot through me.

"Fuck!" shouted Alex. "I knew we shouldn't have trusted her."

"She's fair game for any alpha out there," I said, taking deep breaths.

"I gave her some of my scent blockers," said Jade in a low voice.

"Why?!"

"Sorry," she said.

"There's only one place where she would have gone to," I said. "She's in danger."

Vanessa

"Please, Ophelia," I said.

"It's Queen to you," she replied sharply, straightening her stupid hat. *God, I hated this bitch more than my own evil aunt.* How could she sit there and allow a mother to be separated from her child? She was a narcissist like the rest of the Royal Pack. I briefly wondered how the princess turned out living in the wild with her mountain pack.

"My queen," I said again, trying not to grovel, but I didn't have much of a choice. The guards weren't around, and I didn't need her panicking. If she started yelling and screaming, my time with Gabe would be over instantly. "Before you call anyone, please let me have a moment with my son. How would you feel if you could hold your son for a moment, then have him taken away?"

There. I said it. I had to use everything in my power at this moment.

A flicker of a shadow passed through her eyes. Her dark memories of her miscarriage evident on her face. Her failure to produce more children for the Royal Pack causing her alphas to seek a second omega.

She pursed her lips. "I'll give you a few minutes with your child. Then I don't want to see you again. Ever."

Breathing a sigh of relief, I kissed Gabe on the forehead. I watched warily from the side of my eye as Ophelia settled back in her chair, watching me closely.

"Were you chasing a little butterfly?" I cooed, and he excitedly pointed out the many roses on the ground.

Each moment was precious.

I took in his giggles and stories about his new toys back at the palace. Even though his sentences were choppy, as his mother, I knew exactly what he was trying to say. I sat him on my lap, sitting cross-legged on the grass. I didn't want to ever let him go. I was tempted to take him and run.

I knew I could outrun Ophelia.

But when Ophelia came back, it only felt like a minute. My heart pounded in my chest.

"Alright, that's enough," she said.

"Okay," I said, slowly getting up with Gabe in my arms in anticipation. I had to run through the thicket of palm trees. I knew I could do it. But with a toddler in my arms, it would be hard. "Thank you so much for allowing me to say hi."

While I talked, I slowly backed off from her until I saw her eyes widen. Then I turned and ran, clutching him in my arms.

"Guards, guards!"

I heard her shouts as I ran out of there as quickly as possible without tripping over plants. I had to get out of here.

Heavy footsteps chased me from behind.

I was getting out of breath from carrying Gabe and also recovering from my heat. My body wasn't ready. All the adrenaline in my body was failing me.

My body was weak.

I was too slow.

"Stop right there, lady," shouted a guard, and I could hear the sound of a pistol click.

I stopped in my tracks. I didn't dare risk my life or Gabe's. If they had to kill me for their prince, they wouldn't hesitate. If they got rid of me, Gabe would have no one who truly loved him.

I slowly turned, holding Gabe tight in my arms. Three delta guards surrounded us, pistols drawn. I covered Gabe's eyes. Delta guards were the angriest and the fiercest at the Royal Palace.

Trained to protect at any cost.

"I'm not moving," I said loudly, not daring to move an inch.

"Release the prince," shouted one of the guards. Their faces were covered with a metal helmet that came to their chin with a red stripe on top of it to show that they were Deltas.

I slowly knelt and set Gabe on the floor.

He was crying as soon as I stood back up. I couldn't do anything about it right now. Every move was crucial.

Anything I did right now could determine our future.

"What's going on?" said King Armon, inserting himself into the drama. He took one look at Gabe crying, and he quickly signaled for one of the maids to take him.

"My king," I said, bowing my head. Not looking him in the eyes.

His tall and lanky frame stood over me. He lifted my chin with his finger, making me look at him. He still hadn't shaved his hideous gray goatee—the wrinkles on his face deeper with age.

I couldn't believe I slept with him and the rest of his aging alpha pack. This was the length I'd go to escape my family. In the end, my psychotic aunt was ecstatic that I was sleeping with the kings, imagining her riches.

"Why do you keep coming back?" he said in a low voice. "I know you don't care about your kid. Is it that you miss me? Do you miss our attention?"

"I'm here for my child," I said.

I wasn't going to lose it. I couldn't let him goad me into it.

"Is that the only reason?"

He was looking at me with desire in his eyes. The hunger that all alphas had in them when they lusted after an omega. He was breathing hard as he gazed at me. He could take me as he wished. To play with as he wanted while his pack watched. And I wouldn't have a choice.

"Yes, my king," I whispered, my pulse racing and my head pounding with dread. "Please let me leave with my child, and you'll never see me again."

"Why can't you stay away?" he whispered, bringing his face closer to mine. "My little temptress."

My core began to warm regardless of how I felt about him. He was an alpha male, and I was only an omega. If he wanted me to spread my legs at this very moment, I would be compelled to do it. He was the king of Howl's Edge. I clenched my thighs together.

A shout snapped me out of the spell I was under.

Looking up, I saw Jack and Alex at the front of the pack as they walked toward us. I let out the long breath I was holding. I hadn't felt so small in such a long time. The sight of my seven men gave me courage, and I snickered at Armon.

"Why would you think I'm here for you? That's my pack over there," I said.

Armon looked behind him and snarled at the sight of the seven burly men heading our way. Even Ryan looked extra intimidating today despite his large glasses and flyaway hair. He stopped the maid from entering the palace with Gabe, grabbing him from her. My son looked excited to see Ryan.

The palace guards moved to stand in front of King Armon.

"It's okay, move aside," said Armon to the guards. They moved out of the way, and I was able to see Laurent wink at me. "I want to see what they have to say and if they're here to pick up their disobedient omega."

"Vanessa is our omega," growled Alex, standing before Armon. "And you *will* return Gabe to her."

"I am your king," said Armon in a high voice. "None of you will order me about."

"It's illegal to separate an omega from her child," said Jack, stepping forward.

"I trusted you, Jack," said Armon. "My pack brothers and I trusted you with the location of the omega plant. You were highly esteemed. Are you willing to stoop so low?"

"You're the one who stooped low enough to do this," said Jack. My heart lifted at how firm he was. "My job is to protect my omega. Get the fuck away from her."

Armon stepped away from me, and I could finally breathe without his alpha scent overwhelming me.

"We will revolt, and our families will too," threatened Alex, his red hair wild around his face. "I promise you that if you do not hand over Gabe."

"Listen," said Armon, holding his hands up. "Gabe is the prince of Howl's Edge. He belongs here."

"We can share custody," I said, coming to that realization as long as I was in Howl's Edge. "Please, let me have him on the weekdays."

"We will keep him on the weekends," said Armon. "Is that a deal?"

I felt like my heart was shattering into a million pieces. But it was either this or nothing. I hated this so bad.

"Fine," I said before an alpha could interject and ruin everything. I would be able to take Gabe home with us today. My heart swelled with excitement at the same time. We had managed to do it without a huge revolt from my pack. Without any killing or bloodshed.

"It's a deal," said Alex, shaking hands with King Armon.

Chapter 25

Vanessa

"Gabe hasn't left your side in two days," said Alex as he observed Gabe running in circles in the massive living room of Jack's house.

Ryan, Liam, and Laurent were having an intellectual argument about the world in the kitchen. Mason, Blade, and Jack were playing football in the front yard. I was able to see them from the large window in the living room.

This pack was starting to feel like a family to me.

"He misses me, and I have a feeling he doesn't trust me anymore," I said sadly. I was more than happy to be reunited with my baby now, and I had been in a better mood than I had earlier in the week. But in a couple of days, he would have to return to the Royal Pack for the weekend visit.

I knew it was going to be tough at first, but it was the price I had to pay.

"It's nice to have a baby in the pack again," sighed Alex. "C'mere Gabey boy." Gabe rushed over to Alex in a wind of attack, and Alex chuckled as Gabe tried to tackle him.

"Gabe be nice," I said.

"It's okay, my love," said Alex, kissing me on the cheek. My face burned when he called me that. *Did he really love me?* The only way to know for sure was to be marked by an alpha, and I hadn't gotten that yet. "Aunt Jade will be coming over soon to watch you."

"Woohoo!" said Gabe. He loved Jade ever since Jade decided to spend quite a lot of time coming over here. I even asked her about her job, but she shrugged it off. I hoped she didn't quit her nursing job. I loved that the pack loved Gabe. It made my heart feel full like never before.

"It will give us some mommy and daddy time," whispered Alex, winking at me.

My thighs clenched with desire at his words.

Later that afternoon, Jade had taken Gabe out for ice cream, to his delight.

Immediately after I closed the door, Alex pulled me in close from behind. He started kissing my neck savagely while everyone was out playing football. I knew he wanted one on one attention. For the past few days, I had been distracted and not paying him much attention. It was the first time Gabe was gone from home. Even though I was uneasy about him leaving my side for the first time, I trusted Jade without question.

"Now for the mommy and daddy time," he whispers in my ear. "Do you want daddy to take care of you, baby? It's been a while."

My heart raced, and my pussy clenched with need. Even though I cuddled with the pack at night, I was too scared to have sex with Gabe in the next room. I still wasn't used to having a pack this big, either.

"Yes, daddy alpha," I whispered.

He reached up inside my short skirt and cupped my aching pussy. I was only wearing a thong today. I was feeling extra frisky with every touch from him. His hot breath and hairy skin brushing up on me was making me go crazy. I clutched his shoulders, kissing his lips on my tippy toes.

His red sideburns scratched my face as I kissed him. He pressed his middle finger over my thong, straining to go inside me.

"In the living room?" I squeaked when he pressed his foot between my legs, separating them.

"Daddy alpha will rut you wherever he wants," said Alex sternly. "Now let me feel you. I need to see how ready your little pussy is."

He bent me over the couch, and I felt him pull my thong down over my legs. I stepped out of them, my pussy drenched with slick already. Before he could touch me there, I was trembling with need for his knot. He flipped my skirt over, exposing my butt to the air.

"From the back?" I asked.

"Yes, that's how I'll rut you tonight," he said huskily. It's how he liked it. I kept my head lowered on the couch while waiting for him to touch me. I wiggled my butt teasingly, and he chuckled darkly. "Keep trying to rush me, and you'll be waiting longer for your knot."

I stopped moving.

"Please, daddy alpha," I whispered. My pussy was throbbing, and my core was clenching. "Don't make me wait for your knot."

His hands descended on my ass with a loud smack.

He grasped my butt and spread me open.

"Your pussy is shining in slick," he muttered, gazing long and hard between my legs. My breathing grew rapid with desire. I needed him to touch me. To stop teasing me. Then he plunged a finger deep inside.

"Oh!" I moaned, feeling the thickness of his middle finger inside of me. He started to thrust with his finger, rubbing against my g-spot as he curved his finger inside me. My legs grew weak, and my bottom stuck out further for him. "Please take me."

"Am I your alpha?" he asked, sticking a second finger inside of me. Stretching my pussy. I enjoyed how his fingers slid in and out rapidly inside me. I wanted his cock inside me. His knot more than ever.

"Yes," I said.

"Daddy alpha will fuck you hard in that tight pussy," he said. "Is that what you want, isn't it?"

"Please, daddy alpha," I said, my voice thin compared to his deep baritone voice. He liked to be acknowledged as the leader of the alphas in this pack. "Fuck me hard, daddy alpha."

He released my butt and smacked me across my ass. His fingers glanced over my pussy, and I yelped.

I heard the sound of his belt buckle behind me as it fell to the floor. He straddled me from behind, his hairy thighs pressing against my smooth ones. Then I felt the crown of his thick penis press against my heated slit.

He plunged into my pussy from behind. The feeling of being stretched so wide made my eyes roll back.

"I'm going to rut you now, baby," he said gruffly, pressing his lips to my shoulder. "Like you never felt before."

Bracing myself, I closed my eyes as he began to thrust. Each thrust more powerful than the last.

My entire body was pushed up against the couch cushions as he thrust into me. When the couch began to slide across the floor, he growled.

"Get on the floor," he ordered. "Hands on the ground."

With my orgasm not too far, I quickly complied, moving away from the couch and knelt on the ground on my knees with him still inside me. He gripped my hips as he knelt behind me, his huge body covering mine from the top.

"Is that better, daddy alpha?"

"Much better, sweet thing," he said. "You feel so tight and hot around my cock. I'm going to slam into you now. Get ready."

I felt his raging hot rod inside of me pulsing as he did exactly that. He gripped my hips, so I didn't move or escape.

Then he slammed his cock deep into me.

His groans of pleasure covered the sound of the pack as they surrounded us.

The pack was watching him rut me and take me as his omega. My face heated, but I got hornier as they watched.

"Rut her good," said Mason, pulling off his jeans. I caught sight of his hard-on underneath his boxers, and my pussy clenched wildly around the cock raging inside me. I moaned loudly as I came, shattering around Alex's giant cock.

Then Alex bit me on the back of my shoulder, and I yelped again. He roared as he slammed into me one last time, his cock exploding in a hot stream directly into me. I was panting on my knees by the time he was done rutting and marking me.

His huge cock began to knot at the base, holding us tight together. Filling the void within me. The knot felt so good, along with the burn of the mark on my shoulder.

He officially marked me.

"You all bore witness to the rutting and marking of our omega," he said gruffly, and the men cheered. I suddenly felt closer to them, feeling an odd energy surrounding all of us. Pulling me to them.

"I've never been marked before," I said shakily. "Do you all feel that too?"

"Yes," said Jack, kneeling in front of me and kissing me on the lips. "How do you feel, little omega?"

"Nice and full of knot," I said. The pack chuckled around me.

"I want to take your ass while he's knotted in you," said Mason, his cock bare and purple for all to see.

"Okay," I said. As long as he took his time with me, I was open to it. I loved sexual experimentation. Anything to heighten the experience was more than welcome in my book.

Alex rolled me on top of him while he lay on the ground. His knot was deep and snug inside of me, with no sign of releasing me yet. I laid on top of him with my legs spread on either side of his thighs and my chin resting on his hairy chest.

Alex grasped my butt and spread me open. I felt air hit my secret regions.

"Here you go, Mason," he said, offering my ass to him.

Mason let out an evil chuckle and slid his finger down my crack, pausing against my hole.

"Your tiny bud is clenching," said Mason. "You're trying to act brave, but your ass will tell me the truth."

He pressed around my anus with his finger, and I was still tense.

"Sorry," I said.

"Focus on my touch Vee," he said. "Focus on my little finger rubbing around your asshole. Like this. Around and around. Do you feel it? Let the slick come on its own."

Closing my eyes, I allowed the feeling of his finger press against my ridges go through me. He was hitting my erogenous zones, and I began to clench from arousal again.

Warmth pooled in my belly, and I felt my anus begin to warm and respond to him.

"Spread my ass even more," I said to Alex.

He separated my cheeks wider, and from the side of my eye, I could see Blade recording me on his phone. I blushed, but I stayed focused on Mason fingering my asshole.

His little finger slipped inside me, stretching my hole.

I moaned as I took in the feeling of his finger in my ass while Alex's knot was still buried in my pussy.

Then Mason slowly stretched me with a second finger and a third. Slowly sliding his fingers in and out, using my natural slick as a lubricant.

"Are you ready for my dick?" he asked.

"Yes," I said, my heart pumping with fear and anticipation. I felt the tip of cock soaked in pre-cum jam into my tight hole. I gasped loudly as he pushed inside of me. Inch by inch. Forcing my anus to spread around his cock.

The knot in my pussy and the cock in my ass gave me a feeling of fullness I had never felt before. As I lay on Alex's stomach, Mason pumped into my ass furiously with his thick cock.

"*Fuck yes*," shouted Mason as his thrusts began more wild and savage in my bottom. I was sandwiched between the two alphas. Their scents and pheromones enveloped my senses, making my omega self want to submit fully and be taken. My ass clenched tight around his cock, and I felt more slick seep from my pussy at his every thrust.

"Damn," said Blade, still recording me being taken in the ass while still knotted in my pussy. When Mason came, I felt his hot jets of semen seep into my body, and when his knot swelled inside my anus, I was filled completely.

"Do you like being knotted in both holes?" Mason whispered in my ear. "You dirty little girl."

I knew my cheeks were as red as my hair as he gently bit my earlobe. He settled further inside of me, pushing his knot inside. The huge bulbs on either end stretched me out to the limits.

"Marked, rutted, and knotted," said Jack, watching me as he was sitting on the couch, gripping his cock under his shorts.

"Everything an omega needs," I said, and Alex kissed me hard on the lips. I happily relaxed between the two alphas, absorbing their raw strength and energy of protection around me.

Even though there were seven, they each attended to my different needs that I never thought I needed. Jack was the softer leader of the two, who knew how to get me to do things. Ryan, Liam, and Laurent were the most gentle with me and cared about my emotional well-being the most. They were thoughtful and would sense when I was in distress. Blade and Mason were kinky, fulfilling my most base desires.

And Alex was the daddy of all alphas.

The leader of the home, and he was alpha responsible for my safety.

"I love you," said Alex. Saying the words right out for the first time.

"I love you too," I sighed against his chest, starting to feel his knot inside of me begin to loosen me from its hold.

Epilogue

Vanessa

"T ake the test Vee," said Jack as Alex tried to hand me the pregnancy test.

"Don't be difficult," said Alex.

It had only been two weeks, and I was sure it was too early. They were overreacting.

"I'm not pregnant," I said as Gabe jumped up and down, trying to grab the test.

"If you don't take the test," started Alex. "I will personally sit you down on the toilet and make you pee on it. *While* I'm there."

He sounded serious, with a tone of urgency in his voice.

"Fine," I sighed, knowing he wasn't joking. "It's way too early, but I'll take it. Can someone get Gabe? He's about to poke the cat in the eyes again."

We had gotten Gabe a pet cat to keep him entertained until he had a sibling one day. I wanted a sibling for Gabe.

Especially now that I was settled in with a pack. I made my way into the bathroom on the first floor of the house and locked the door.

After taking the test, I heard a knock on the bathroom door. I rolled my eyes. They were so impatient.

"Did you take it?" asked Alex.

"Yes," I called. "We need to wait three minutes."

I washed my hands and carried the test out of the bathroom.

I set it on the dresser, and Alex already had his timer on his phone, counting down the minutes.

My heart was pumping with anticipation and excitement.

I actually had some cramping the other day, which Jade told me was a sign of pregnancy. Jade knew her stuff as a nurse. It boggled my mind that she didn't like her job. As an omega, that was a hard feat to accomplish. Without a pack for protection, I struggled on Howl's Edge. Living with the humans, I was able to be free and do my own thing. It felt nice while it lasted.

The timer went off, and my heart beat like rapid fire.

I watched as Alex picked up the test from the dresser, his eyes wide as he stared at it.

"What does it say?" I asked, my heart sinking as I still sat on the edge of the bed.

"It's positive," he said slowly, dropping the test. His face broke into a wide smile, and my heart felt like it would burst with happiness.

"For real?" asked Jack, looking at me with new wonder in his eyes.

"We did it," said Mason. "Our sperm is strong as fuck. On the first heat cycle too."

"Oh goodness," I said, laughing as Alex carried me in a bear hug. Gabe jumped in, too, pulling my shirt. Then the rest of the men crowded in a huge group hug, with Laurent lifting Gabe in the air. Tears pricked at my eyes, shocked that this was happening to me. I was pregnant with a pack who loved me.

These men would do anything for me, and I knew I was one lucky omega.

It was Saturday, and dropping Gabe off at the palace was the hardest part of my week. Blade was driving the car, and Gabe sat next to me in his car seat, asking me a ton of questions.

Gabe was thriving in Howl's Edge.

He was able to run free a whole lot more than we were in the human lands. He was mostly outside playing on the sand or in the water. As a mother, that made me happy to see.

I touched my belly, unable to wait for my baby to grow. I loved everything about pregnancy, except when I was sick in the morning. The men were super helpful in the mornings. Jack had begged me not to leave the house today, but I was going to see Gabe off. No matter what anyone said.

So even if I felt a little queasy, I had to come here.

Jack, Alex, Liam, and Ryan were off handling the heat suppressant plants and training. So it was just myself, Blade, Mason, and Laurent hanging out for today. I wanted to spend more time with them, so it was good.

"Alright, little buddy," said Blade, parking in front of the palace. "Don't take forever chitchatting, Vee."

"I'll do whatever I want, my love," I said, kissing him on the cheek. His face turned pink, and I smiled as I stepped out of the car. The men talked a big game, but inside, they were softies for love. "Just don't leave me."

He smirked, and I scowled, closing the door behind me.

I opened the passenger side door and helped Gabe out of his seat. Holding his hand, we walked towards the palace, and the guards let us in without question. Upon entering, the first person I saw was Princess Lyra and her son Manny with yogurt all over his hands, with a maid chasing him all over the place. Only her alpha, Luke, accompanied her with her visits to the palace. Her sigma husbands didn't get along with the kings, according to her, so they stayed back in the remote part of the island.

The princess smiled upon seeing Gabe.

She held her arms out, and he rushed into them. She was his half-sister, after all. We were cordial but not too friendly. I had a feeling she still held something against me.

"Gabe!" she exclaimed. "Vanessa, how are you doing?"

"Well, I got some news this week," I said, unable to hold back my smile. A knowing look came over her eyes.

"You're pregnant?" she squealed.

"Yes," I said, fully smiling now.

"Oh my gosh, we need to have a birth celebration," she said.

"Oof, that's a lot of work," I said, shaking my head. My hand was on my belly even though there wasn't much of a bump yet.

"It'll be fun, and you deserve it."

"Not really," I said. "Did you forget what I did to you?"

"That was in the past. We need to move on," she said. My mom and I are happy that you found your pack. I have a little brother now who's also best friends with my son, Manny."

"I just want to say I'm sorry," I said. "I never said it out loud and wanted you to know it."

She walked over to me with Gabe in her arms and hugged me.

"I forgive you, Vanessa," said Lyra. "Don't get haunted by the past, okay?"

"Thank you," I said. "Alright, I'll think about this whole birth celebration thing."

"Don't worry, I'll help you organize it with Jade," she said, smiling. "Jade can get her friends too. It'll be huge!"

Once I was back in the car, Blade could tell something was up by the way I was smiling and daydreaming about the birth celebration. And the baby.

"What's going on, my love?" he asked, squeezing my thigh as he drove.

"Lyra and I were just talking about making a birth celebration for me when the baby's born," I said, rubbing my belly.

"Aw man, I hate parties," he said. I couldn't imagine Blade at a party and being a social butterfly. The thought made me giggle. He was far from that, so I understood why he was grumpy about the idea.

When we reached the pack house, Blade held my hand as we walked up the driveway and to the front door. As we walked inside, I saw a big three-tier cake with white frosting all over it on the dining room table. Laurent was smiling proudly behind it. Mason was doing pushups in the living room.

"Oh!" I squealed. "What's the cake for?"

"I got it to celebrate our positive pregnancy test," said Laurent.

"I'm trying to get some exercise in before I try that dangerous stuff," panted Mason, sweat beading off his forehead. He was shirtless, his back bare and his muscles visibly straining.

"Mason, you can have a cheat day occasionally," I laughed.

"No, babe," he grunted, doing more reps.

"Shit, I ain't waiting for him," said Laurent, slicing into the cake. We each grabbed our plate of cake and sat around the dining table, discussing the birth celebration plans and the baby.

"Do you want a boy or a girl?" I asked them.

"Girl," they all said at the same time. I suddenly remembered the child they had lost. The little three-year-old girl. My heart ached for them. Every other night, we'd go to their old house to visit the ocean gravestone. Doing that has brought me closer to them and their tragedy.

"But a boy is fine too," said Mason hastily, his lips covered in frosting.

"Blade honey, you only took one bite," I said, finishing up my slice. I was craving a sweet today, and this hit the spot for me.

"I'm waiting until you're done."

"Why?!"

"So I can eat my slice from your ass," he said.

I blinked in shock.

"Are you serious?"

"Dead serious. Take off your panties, baby," said Blade, watching me.

"This is the craziest thing you ever asked me," I said, pursing my lips. "Can't you just eat your cake like a normal person?"

"Baby, take your panties off," he said, his voice husky. My pulse began to pound like crazy. I wanted it, too, despite my protests. I secretly enjoyed it when the alphas got frustrated with me.

Blade

She was teasing me.

Vanessa lifted her dress, showing off her light blue panties. She slowly rolled it down, her eyes looking at us teasingly. A small sexy smile on her face.

"Like this?" she asked.

"Take it off, Vee," I ordered, getting impatient. I could smell her scent getting stronger as she pulled her panties off. She stepped out of them and looked at me expectantly. "Give your panties to me."

Taking them from her, I saw the wet stain on the seat of it. I licked my lips and threw the panties to Mason, the creep. He sniffed the panties wholeheartedly.

"Smells amazing," Mason whispered, pressing the blue panties to his nose tightly. Vanessa stared at him with wide eyes.

I caught him numerous times going through the dirty laundry, looking for her underwear as he masturbated, so this was the perfect treat for him. Next, I grabbed my plate of cake and added another giant slice to it.

I placed it on the edge of the table.

"Get on the table. Let me carry you," I said, approaching her. Her candy scent washed over me as I lifted her by the legs and plopped her on the wooden table. "Take off your dress, baby."

"I don't think this is necessary," she said, lifting her dress.

"Oh, it's very necessary," said Laurent, helping her remove her dress. He wasn't as expressive as us when it came to fucking her, but he was always more than willing to join our group activities.

I had no problem taking the initiative.

I unsnapped her bra, and it tumbled down to the chair. Her ample breasts bounced when I did that. My cock was so hard right now I couldn't fucking think straight. I wanted to fuck her so bad with cake inside of her.

"I want you to sit on the cake, baby," I said. Her face reddened as she turned her back to me, showing off her shapely ass. She squatted over the cake. "Lower yourself." I watched with bated breath as she slowly lowered her ass onto the cake.

"It's cold," she complained.

"Shh," I said, spreading her ass cheeks wide as she sat on the cake. She wiggled over the cake, getting the frosting smeared all around her butt. She looked delicious as she looked back at us, her eyes wide. Her frosted butt was hanging in the air, ready for me to devour. My balls tightened, and I could feel my pre-cum leaking into my boxers. "Kneel for us, so we can take a look at your bottom."

Vanessa went on her hands and knees, showing off her ass.

"Bounce that ass," said Laurent, turning on the music. She wiggled on the table, showing off her dance moves. My cock was getting harder the more I watched her gyrate her ass back and forth. Making it clap wildly.

I could tell she wasn't lying when she mentioned she was a dancer before. We alphas were enraptured by her butt as she bounced up and down on the table, moving those hips. I grasped her hips, holding her still.

"It's time for me to have a taste," I said. I grasped her left ass cheek, and Mason grabbed her right. We gently spread her open, and Laurent smeared more frosting down her crack. "Good girl."

"Mhm," she moaned as she felt Laurent's fingers slide up and down her bottom and cover her pussy with frosting. Her entire nether region was covered in white frosting, her pussy area glistening with her slick. "I want to be your good girl."

"Then go on your elbows, baby," I said. "I need a closer inspection."

She complied, and I admired how her pussy and asshole twitched as we held her open. I couldn't wait to get a taste of her. Bringing my face near her ass, I slowly licked her left cheek, the sweetness of the frosting hitting my tongue. Mason did the same on her other cheek, and Laurent began licking her pussy.

"This is *real* dessert," said Mason, his voice muffled against her ample cheek.

My tongue ventured to her crack. I heard her intake of breath as I licked her up and down her crack, swallowing the frosting and the taste of her slick. I let Mason take a turn licking the rest of the frosting from her ass crack.

His tongue was wide, covering every inch of the middle of her bottom.

I watched her pink flesh shiver as Laurent licked off the frosting from her pussy. Her pussy was shiny with Laurent's licking and her own copious amount of slick she was releasing.

Our omega was more than ready to get fucked in her holes.

Her anus twitched and clenched every time Mason swiped his tongue over it.

"Lick our pregnant omega harder," I said, removing my sweatpants and boxers in a hurry as I watched them lick her frantically. Trying to get her all juices. "My turn."

Mason moved his face to continue licking her cheek as I took over her ass crack. I pressed my tongue against her anus, feeling it open under my tongue. Laurent's tongue was already deep into her pussy as she moaned on the table.

She stuck her bottom out further.

I loved when our little kitten did that. She was getting heated up, arching her back like that for us. Laurent plunged his tongue into her pussy over and over while Mason pushed his tongue into her anus next.

"Oh my god," she shouted, trembling on the table. Her thighs were shaking by the time she rode down her orgasm.

"All clean now," I said, patting her bottom. "Now it's time to fuck that tight bottom of yours."

"Be gentle!" she shouted as I carried her to the couch. She got into a kneeling position again, and I stood on the couch over her. My cock was dangling and ready to fuck her in the ass.

"We'll both take her pussy," said Laurent.

I smiled when she yelped and tried to get away, but I held her bottom tight.

"If they both knot inside me, it'll hurt!"

"You're not getting away, little omega," I said with an evil grin. "But don't worry, we'll stop if it hurts too much." I could smell how horny she was getting with every minute. She didn't have Jack or Ryan around to protect her. She was in the hands of the creepiest team of alphas.

"Spread your legs and hold your bottom open," ordered Mason. When she hesitated, he prodded her thighs with his hard cock to hurry.

She widened her knees on the couch and gripped her ass cheeks open for me.

"Good girl," I cooed, and she let out a happy whimper. She loved praises. "Let the daddies take charge of you now, baby. Be a good girl and spread your ass wider for me."

I lined up my cock to her clenching anus dripping in slick. I rubbed the head of my dick over her ridges, covering the circle of her dark hole in pre-cum. Laurent's large dark cock pressed against her pussy, rubbing against her clit until she moaned.

"We'll go in at the same time," said Mason, also bringing his cock to the entrance of her pussy. We lined up our cocks, ready to penetrate at the same time. Vanessa wiggled her bottom.

"So slow," she said to our ire. "You talk a big game."

"Should we fuck the attitude out of our omega?" I said, my cock ready to pounce into her little ass. It was dancing and twitching outside her entrance, eager to go in.

"Let's do this," said Mason.

My cock was too big for her anus as I tried to push the tip inside of her. She was resisting me, clenching her butt repeatedly. I squeezed in another inch and used my finger to rub around her hole, feeling her sphincter to loosen her up. Mason and Laurent were trying to shove their huge cock into her pussy at the same time while I hovered above her, standing on the couch and taking her ass. They were pressed up against the couch, jamming their cock into her.

She gasped out loud when we all pushed in deeper.

One cock in her ass. Two in her pussy.

"Do you like this?" I growled in her ear as she gripped the edge of the couch. She was listening to me intently, her face pink. "Huh, baby? Do you like three big alpha cocks inside of you?"

"Yes," she breathed, her eyes rolling back in her head as she arched her back.

I felt her tight ass clenching on my cock, covered in her slick as I thrust in and out of her. Laurent and Mason had a rhythm going on below as they pounded into her pussy at the same time and gripped her thighs, holding her open as she faced away from us.

I cupped her breasts, squeezing each time I thrust into her ass.

I enjoyed hearing the moans roll off her tongue. The way she couldn't get control of the situation. She was under the mercy of our cocks right now. Squeezing her ample breasts, I pistoned deep into her ass until she screamed my name.

"Yes, good girl," I said. "Clench your anus for me, baby."

"I can't," she said, gasping. "It's already so tight, and my pussy is so full."

"If you want to be a good girl. Clench for me," I said a little harder. When I felt her anus grip my cock even tighter, I lost control. I pounded into her ass like no tomorrow. Hot warmth slid up and down my fucking cock. Heating my cock thoroughly. The pressure of her hold squeezed my cock into submission. Before long, I came hard into her ass, my cum shooting inside of her. "Fuck."

The relief of my cock knotting inside her felt so good as I finished in her ass. Hot cum squirted around her anus, spilling all over the couch. *Damn, Jack is going to kill me.* As I knotted inside her ass, I rested above her, waiting for Laurent and Mason.

I watched their cocks disappear into her pussy, thrusting into her simultaneously while she gasped each time.

"Your pussy is so beautiful," said Laurent.

I enjoyed watching our little omega getting fucked by the others. It was sexy to watch as their cocks pressed into her pussy over and over. I even kept my little video of her getting rutted by our pack leader for my personal needs.

"Fuck!" shouted Mason as he finished.

Laurent followed soon after, and she groaned as both cocks began to knot inside of her. I rubbed her shoulders and whispered sweet words into her ear while she took our knots.

"Good job, baby," said Laurent, kissing her on her back. She nodded limply and smiled. Mason rubbed her belly, and I kissed her neck.

"Who knew what a little cake could bring," she joked, trying to catch her breath.

"Sexy times, baby," said Laurent.

"You did an amazing job," I said, absorbing her scent as I pressed my lips against her collarbone.

She was our omega, making us complete again after so many years. I would do anything to keep a smile on her face and to keep her thoroughly fucked at all times of the day.

"I vow to keep you happy, Vee," I said.

"You already have," she whispered, turning her head and kissing me.

Ten Months Later
Vanessa

Wearing an all-white flowy dress, I held my baby girl Lacy in my arms as I waited for the right moment to step outside. A crowd was outside, waiting for me to show my baby to the world.

It was the birth celebration.

Jack and Alex stood on either side of me, wearing black suits, now co-leaders of the pack. The rest of the pack surrounded me from behind, wearing matching blue suits. I swallowed, tucking the little white blanket under Lacy's chin.

"I smell your nervousness," said Jack, gripping my elbow in support. "You look absolutely stunning, baby."

"Thank you," I said in a low voice. "I hope I don't do anything stupid. I'm not one to be graceful."

"Remember you have our love and support every step of the way," said Ryan from behind me. He rubbed my back softly. "Nothing you do will be embarrassing."

"Is it time now?" asked Mason. "I want to get this party over with so we can cuddle Vee and the baby later."

"Mhm, that sounds very appealing," said Alex, kissing Lacy on the cheek. "I want to ditch this party too."

"No, we're doing this," I said sternly. "We have all the time in the world to cuddle. Just behave nicely with the other packs and be nice. No rivalry, okay?"

"Alright, it's time," said Jack, opening the front door. Jack and Alex walked out first to the cheering of the crowd.

As soon as I stepped out of the house, the crowd erupted in cheers and clapping. Music blared from every corner of the large front yard. I smiled, surrounded and protected by my pack, as I lifted Lacy in the air for the crowd to see. My core was still weak, but I was gaining strength every day.

"Ahhh," said the ladies when they saw my little bundle.

I was so proud of my baby. She didn't cry at all as I hugged her to me. She was quietly observing her surroundings at one-month-old. Her hair was bright red like Alex's and mine. Her nose was regal and straight.

One by one, the packs with their omegas came to congratulate me. Jade introduced her friends Keera and Tiana, who showed up with their packs. Children ran everywhere, chasing each other down or trying to get into the huge pool despite an adult guarding it.

"Congratulations," said Keera, who had long black hair and wearing a strapless red dress. "This is my pack, and this is Jatix."

Her pack leader had straight white hair with the most intense purple eyes I'd ever seen.

"Congratulations," said Jatix, shaking Alex's hand and the rest of my pack. I noticed he also had a delta in his pack, and Liam naturally gravitated toward him. Soon they were both laughing and sharing stories from what I could hear.

"She's the cutest little thing," said Tiana, touching Lacy's hair. "Congratulations. Having a baby always changes the dynamics of a family."

Tiana wore a lovely emerald dress, and her hair was curled around her shoulders. Her brown eyes looked kind.

"It does," I said. "It feels more like a family. The house feels full and cozier."

"She described it right," said Keera smiling.

"This is Grant, my pack leader," said Tiana, grabbing her alpha's hand and pulling him over to me to say hi.

There were so many people at the party I felt a little overwhelmed, but I smiled graciously as I shook Grant's hand. He was built like a linebacker with rich brown skin and curly black hair that shined under the bright sun. He was well put together.

Jack scowled as he saw me shake Grant's hand, and I couldn't help but let out a giggle.

"Congratulations," said Grant in his deep voice. "I remember the day we had our twins like it was yesterday."

"Thank you," I said, laughing as Jack placed himself in front of me. He wasn't discreet at all.

"Lots of alpha energy around here," said Keera.

"Let's go to the fancy chairs I set up," said Jade proudly, leading us toward them. Jade was wearing a feathered blue skirt with a plain blue shirt. She looked colorful and lively.

There were several chairs covered in white cloth with gold bows in the back of them, set in a large circle around tables of food.

"You did an amazing job," I said, unable to take my eyes off her handiwork.

"Way more fun than nursing," she said jovially.

I sat between Keera and Tiana as Jade ran off to bring me some food. More ladies and packs came to congratulate me, coming over to where I sat in the chair. There was a pile of gifts covered in glittering pink paper sitting on a table against the wall of Jack's mansion. I never had anything special done like this for me, and tears immediately sprung to my eyes.

"Oh no, what's wrong?" asked Tiana, touching my arm.

"I can hold Lacy for a bit," said Keera quickly, and I carefully set her in Keera's arms.

Tiana handed me a tissue, and I gently dabbed my tears away, trying not to smear my mascara.

"I'm just so happy," I said. "Believe it or not, I never had a birthday growing up or anything special done for me. I'm glad you guys came."

"Of course," said Tiana. "I wouldn't miss this at all. If you're Jade's friend, we're all friends."

"Sorry, I didn't mean to bring the mood down," I said.

Keera placed a calming hand on my other arm. "Don't apologize. Omegas don't have it easy, you know. I was auctioned off, just like you. Jade told me your story."

"But aren't you a doctor?" I asked incredulously. I couldn't believe she had also been auctioned to her pack and managed to find true love.

"Not everything is what it seems," she said, smiling warmly. "I was lucky it was Jatix who chose me. If it had been anyone else, I doubt I would be where I am today."

A boy who looked to be seven years old came up to Keera, and he stared at the baby.

"Is that your son?" I asked.

"Yep, Lio, say hi to the ladies. Don't be rude," said Keera, hugging him to her and kissing him on the cheek.

"Hi," he said, looking embarrassed and looking back down at the baby. "She's cute."

"Isn't she?" said Keera. It made my heart warm to see him touch Lacy's hand.

"Looks like the party started already," said Princess Lyra, making her way through everyone towards me.

She was holding Gabe and Manny's hands who each had red lollipops in their other hands. Lyra had on a fancy purple dress with teardrop earrings, her blond hair piled high on her head.

"The princess is here too?" asked Tiana, incredulously staring at the princess. "She's always dressed to impress."

"She's my son's half-sister," I explained. Then, when Tiana looked confused, I chuckled. "It's a long story."

Lyra had volunteered to watch Gabe at the castle while Jade and my pack prepared everything for the party. When I tried to help, Jade wouldn't hear of it, so I stayed with Lacy in the house the entire time.

"Oh dear, the men are playing football," said Keera amused, watching her delta throw a football in the air with his massive strength. The men would constantly look over at their omega to see if we saw any impressive moves they made.

After we ate food, talked, and gossiped some more- it was time for pictures. I carried Lacy as Jade tried to position my pack around me perfectly. Alex and Jack were on either side of me, with Gabe directly in front of me. The rest of my pack fanned out around us, and I tried to smile for every picture. It was tough to keep a smile on all day, especially when a camera was on me. It wasn't like when Blade recorded me getting rutted by Alex. My face heated at the memory, and I knew in half of my pictures, my face was probably red.

"So cute!" shouted Jade as she looked at the photos. She was the only single omega in this entire gathering who wasn't matched to a pack. I hoped one day she would find a pack who adored her.

"You're so beautiful," said Alex, kissing me. Everyone who saw us let out whoops and cheers.

"And we love you," said Jack, kissing my cheek. "I saw you crying earlier. Why were you crying?"

"This all feels special to me," I said. "You can call it tears of joy."

Laurent brushed the side of my face with his finger. "We understand, sweetheart."

"I swear once this day is over, I'm making love to you," growled Alex in my ear.

My center clenched in desire.

I couldn't wait for him either. For all of them. And that was all I ever wanted. No amount of power or riches in the world would ever fill the void I had before.

A pack who adored me. A pack who cared.

THE END

Continue on reading to **Book 5! Matched to the Pack**, featuring **Jade**!

Don't forget to leave a review!
It helps authors like me keep producing more stories for you.
Thank you so much! <3

Also By Layla Sparks

Howl's Edge Island: Omega For The Pack Series (Reverse Harem Series)

Book 1: Stolen by The Pack

Book 2: Auctioned to the Pack

Book 3: Princess For The Pack

Book 4: Betrayed by The Pack

Book 5: Matched to The Pack

Captive After Moonlight Series: DARK Romance

Jenna gets a lot more than she can handle when visiting the smutty toy shop downtown. She looks for the perfect naughty toy, but little does she know that a werewolf is looking for *his* toy...

Now she's kidnapped by a psycho HOT werewolf who believes Jenna should be his.

Book 1: Werewolf's Mate

Book 3: Werewolf's Captive

Five Sexy Bigfoot Short Stories: Kink For Monsters

Book: Five Sexy Bigfoot Short Stories

Alien Erotica Series: Tantalizing Tentacles of Korynz: (Kidnapping & Age Gap)

Book 1: Disciplined by My Alien Teacher

Book 2: Examined by My Alien Doctor

Book 3: Enslaved by The Alien King

Satisfying Bigfoot's Nightly Desires

Start the 5-book completed romance erotica series now. You will not want to miss this hot adventure ;)

Book 1: Bigfoot's Captive

Book 2: Bigfoot's Mate

Book 3: *Bigfoot's Love*

Book 4: *Bigfoot's Proposal*

Book 5: *Bigfoot's Vow*

Desires of The Merman

Looking for some underwater sexy action? Start this completed 3 book series now!

Book 1: *The Merman's Vow*

Book 2: *The Merman's Baby*

Book 3: *The Merman's Mate*

The Suitors & The Vampire Prince

The Suitors & The Vampire Prince

A hot historical romance if you're looking for a longer read. A queen is looking for the perfect suitor but she must sleep with them first. Which suitor is up to the challenge??

Thank you so much for reading!

Please leave a review letting me know your favorite parts of the story. This helps authors like me keep producing more stories for you. To get updates on my next book and to get exclusive cover reveals and first chapters, sign up for my newsletter below:

Newsletter: https://authorlaylasparks.wixsite.com/layla-sparks

Tiktok: @author_laylasparks
Instagram: https://www.instagram.com/author_laylasparks/
Twitter: https://twitter.com/LaylaSparks7
Facebook Group (interact with other readers!) Layla's Steamy Facebook Group
Youtube: https://youtube.com/@laylasparks

Printed in Great Britain
by Amazon

29858741R00108